sisters of the heart

best buddies

iFLOAT

soul sister

friends forever

kindred spirits

sister-friends

SISTERCHICKS
in Gondolas!

girlfriends

pals for life

chum

confidante

gal pals

true blue

a sisterchick® novel

SISTERCHICKS
in Gondolas!

ROBIN JONES GUNN

Multnomah® Publishers *Sisters, Oregon*

SISTERCHICKS IN GONDOLAS!
published by Multnomah Publishers, Inc.

© 2006 by Robin's Ink, LLC
International Standard Book Number: 1-59052-505-1

Sisterchicks is a trademark of Multnomah Publishers, Inc.

Cover image of women by Kim McElroy Photography
Background cover image by Pete Turner/Getty Images

Unless otherwise indicated, Scripture quotations are from:
The Holy Bible, New King James Version (NKJV)
© 1984 by Thomas Nelson, Inc.
Other Scripture quotations are from:
The Message by Eugene H. Peterson
© 1993, 1994, 1995, 1996, 2000
Used by permission of NavPress Publishing Group
All rights reserved.

Multnomah is a trademark of Multnomah Publishers, Inc.
and is registered in the U.S. Patent and Trademark Office.
The colophon is a trademark of Multnomah Publishers, Inc.

Printed in the United States of America

For information:
MULTNOMAH PUBLISHERS, INC.
601 N. LARCH STREET
SISTERS, OR 97759
Library of Congress Cataloging-in-Publication Data

Gunn, Robin Jones, 1955-
Sisterchicks in gondolas! / Robin Jones Gunn.
     p. cm.
ISBN 1-59052-505-1
1. Women travelers--Fiction. 2. Female friendship--Fiction. 3.
Venice (Italy)--Fiction. I. Title.
PS3557.U4866S5628 2006
813'.54--dc22

                                        2006006118

06 07 08 09 10—10 9 8 7 6 5 4 3 2 1

For two amazing Sisterchicks I met thirty years ago:

Ruby, my bunk bed mate in our dorm room in Austria
back when our hair was its original color.
Cooking with you last summer in our Venetian palace
was golden. I love the way we can always pick up
our conversations where we left off, no matter how many
years or miles have filled the pauses.

And Kate, my sister-in-law, who loved me from day one.
I love you back, more than I ever show.
Thanks for being more than a relative;
you are a true friend and a Sisterchick forever.

"God, my shepherd! I don't need a thing.
You have bedded me down in lush meadows,
you find me quiet pools to drink from.
True to your word, you let me catch my breath
and send me in the right direction....
My cup brims with blessing."

PSALM 23:1–3, 5B (THE MESSAGE)

Prologue

I *don't think* I would have gone to Venice if I hadn't had a crazy thought five years ago that woke me at three o'clock one morning.

I was used to wacky, middle-of-the-night thoughts, but not like this one. Usually I created mental memos such as, "Send Aunt Becky's birthday card by Tuesday, or it won't arrive in time." In my head I would respond, "Okay," and fall back asleep.

Other times the thoughts came fragmented like, "car insurance." Those were the ones I hated because I'd lie alone in the darkness wondering, "Am I behind on a payment? Or was I merely dreaming about a late-night commercial with some dancing lizard telling me I was paying too much for my current coverage?"

When I discussed these annoying, sleep-robbing thoughts with my sister-in-law, Sue, she responded,

"Welcome to menopause." Then she told me that she keeps a notepad and pen by her bed and another one in her purse at all times. "That way, if I do go completely insane, at least I'll have left a trail for the medical community to follow, sort of like bread crumbs."

Taking her advice, I put a notepad by my bed. That's why I can still remember the persistent thought that woke me and set this adventure into motion. The 3 a.m. revelation was simple: "You're not done yet."

That was it. I wasn't "done." Done with what, I didn't know.

I wrote down the thought, but then, instead of falling back to sleep, I considered all the things I had started but never finished. The list was long. Very few events in my life had unfurled the way I had thought they would. I was too old to start over but too young to roll over and play dead. Such is the muddle of midlife, I told myself. I shouldn't elevate my expectations this far along in my quota of years. I should be winding down, right?

But at 3 a.m. that particular spring morning, I wasn't "done" yet. And I didn't know what that meant.

Sleep wouldn't return, so I slipped out of bed and made a cup of tea. The sound of the newspaper thumping against the front door of my condo told me the world around me was waking. In a few hours I would leave for work. During the hectic pace of my position as a checkout clerk at Abbot's Grocery, I would scan dozens of cans of soup and tomato sauce. I would weigh Red Delicious apples (code #4782) and dripping bundles of romaine lettuce (code #4623). I would say, "Have a nice day" more times than any human should have to say that phrase, and I would forget any thoughts that had come to me in the night.

Then, in the wee hours of the next morning, the same thought returned and woke me again. This time I sat up in bed and said aloud, "What? What isn't finished?" All was silent except for the whirl of the ceiling fan over my bed.

I fell back asleep. My unremarkable life continued at its usual pace for two more weeks.

Then a letter came from Sam, a friend from college who was now the director of an international mission that was based in Europe.

> *Jenna, would you consider traveling to Venice in July? We need someone to cook at our mission leaders' retreat. You keep coming to mind. We were given two comp airline tickets from the U.S. so you can bring a friend. The retreat is only for four days. You may stay at the palace the remainder of the week at no charge. Please respond ASAP.*

I read the note again. Venice? Why me? Why now?

I wasn't a very good cook. Sam knew that because I worked on the kitchen staff one summer at a camp he and his wife ran in Austria. But that was during college. A lifetime ago. Sam and Austria and cooking all happened when

I was young and naive and had lofty plans for my life. Then I fell in love, and, ignoring advice from friends and family, I spontaneously got married. I had a beautiful daughter and an unwanted divorce all before I was twenty-seven. That was when my life grew small.

Now I was being invited to be part of something outside the small boundaries of my broken, limited life. And in Europe, no less. Was this the unfinished business?

Sam's invitation stirred something deep within me. I realized that no matter what age we are, a profound sweetness glides over the human spirit when we are included in a small circle by an old friend. It's a humbling thing to be chosen.

I cried for the first time in a long time, and then I called my sister-in-law. Sue was the friend I chose to take with me to Italy.

She was coming up for air after the worst two years of her life. Because she never had been to Europe, she understandably was hesitant about leaving home, but she finally agreed. We left behind everything familiar about our lives in Dallas when we boarded that airplane and flew to Italy.

Neither of us expected the transformations that began in us during our week in Venice. Our luxurious makeovers started with morning walks to the *panetteria,* where we bought our daily bread. Our nails were "manicured" by eager pigeons that we fed from open hands at San Marco

Square. Instead of cucumber slices over closed eyes, we opened our eyes wide inside the grand, Byzantine churches and drew in the scent of honeyed candles. We meditated on God and life while listening for the echo of footsteps on the ancient tiles.

So much changed inside both of us on that trip. Sue and I look back and refer to that summer as the summer we were ambushed. Neither of us saw the blessings coming. They just came—and kept coming—and bowled us over.

Sue now has a term for what happened in Venice. She says we were "victims of grace." I like that. Both of us had been victims of a lot of other stuff over the long years. How sweet of God to make us victims of grace when we were old enough to appreciate what that gift cost Him.

Yes, we were transformed in Venice. We both are convinced that what happened to us never would have happened in Dallas. Not that God can't change a heart and a life in Dallas—or anywhere else—but they don't have gondolas in Dallas. And for our transformation, we definitely needed a gondola.

One

From the minute—and I do mean the very minute—that Sue and I exited the Santa Lucia train terminal an unexpected sense of confidence filled me. My journeys during college had taken me all over Europe with only a backpack and a list of the low-priced youth hostels. But I'd never come here, to *Venezia*, the city that Italy wears proudly like a diamond-studded broach on the cuff of her tall boot.

I led the way down the steps and into the open plaza on the edge of the Grand Canal, feeling like a wayward daughter who had finally come home. Venezia in all her morning glory rushed to greet my senses like a big, fat Italian mama holding out her tawny arms in a welcome.

Sue, however, dipped her chin and gazed at Venice the way one respectfully smiles upon the elderly, not sure whether to sit or to stand in their presence.

"That must be where we buy tickets for the *vaporetto*," I said, forging ahead to the ticket booth. Sue let me do the talking as I bought our passage for the floating public transportation that would take us to the corner of Venice where we would stay for the next week.

"Do you have the map?" Sue rifled through her shoulder bag.

"Right here." I handed it over.

Sue unfolded the map, and I drew in a deep breath of glimmering morning air.

"It's not the way I thought it would be," Sue said, looking at the map and looking up at the buildings across the canal.

"How did you think Venice would be?"

"Well, not so old and run-down, I guess."

"I think that's part of her charm."

"Her?" Sue questioned.

"Yes," I said unapologetically. "Her."

Sue shot me a skeptical glance as our vaporetto pulled into the dock. We boarded along with a string of locals and a few luggage-lugging tourists. The built-in bench seats on the floating bus were occupied, so Sue and I stood beside a young man who was wearing a pressed and starched chef's jacket.

I pulled sunglasses from my shoulder bag and set my gaze on the welcoming sight of the sun-baked block buildings.

"I didn't have enough time to check the map and see where our stop is," Sue said. "Do you think it's very far from here? Do you remember?"

"Yes, I remember. It's not far."

Sue leaned to the side, resting her hand on her luggage and looking as if she was trying hard to appear relaxed.

Another young man, also in a chef's jacket, hurried to catch our vaporetto before we left the dock. The late arriver greeted the man beside me with a handshake and a rousing, *"Buon giorno!"* The two men stood close, shoulders back, hands in motion, as they exchanged an animated dialogue of staccato words. I loved eavesdropping on them even though I couldn't understand anything they said.

As the vaporetto began its journey down the Grand Canal, a cool breeze set to work, stitching white lace to the crests of the calm waters.

"Isn't this gorgeous?" I murmured more to myself than to Sue.

"Do you want me to take a picture?" Sue dug into a zippered pouch of her suitcase. "Maybe we could ask someone to take a picture of both of us? How's my hair? Is it a fright?"

Sweet Sue's pomegranate red hair was not only her most noticeable asset but also sometimes her greatest liability. This morning a gaggle of wayward rouge-hued strands had taken flight and were veering off in a variety of directions, conducting their own unguided tours of eye-level Venice.

"It could use some attention," I said delicately. "Don't worry about the pictures. We'll have plenty of chances later."

Sue smoothed her hand over the top of her head, as she tried to assess the damage inflicted by our all-night flight. Reaching into her pocket, she pulled out a hairclip and wrestled with her tangles.

I tucked a few flipped tails of my low-maintenance, unmemorable brown hair behind my ears and noticed an older woman standing across from us who was intrigued with the way Sue was taming her personal shrew. The woman had been in line behind us at the ticket booth. I smiled, but she had her gaze fixed on Sue.

We motored past an unending row of personality-plus buildings that lined the Grand Canal. Most of the four-story boxes were painted in muted earth tones. They showed off their comely window arches, intricate balconies, and deep plaster gashes with as much pride as any soldier who had been wounded and decorated after battle. Clearly, these brave, still-standing offspring of Venezia had earned their medals of honor for years of faithful service and courage in the line of duty.

"*Ca'd'Oro?*" The older woman tapped Sue on the arm. "*Avete un biglietto di Ca'd'Oro?*"

Sue's stunned expression gave away that she had no idea what the woman was asking. Blessedly, the clean-scrubbed chef leaned toward us with a chin-up gesture and asked, "Do you want Ca'd'Oro?"

"Oh, y'all speak English!" Sue turned into her charming Southern self.

"Yes, of course. Do you want Ca'd'Oro? It's the next stop. She is saying you bought tickets for Ca'd'Oro."

His accent was mesmerizing. I wanted to say "what?" just so he would keep talking to us. But I knew Ca'd'Oro was the name of the stop where we were supposed to disembark. And, apparently, so did the woman with the keen eye for details.

"Yes, this is our stop," I said. "Thanks for your help."

"Yes, thanks, y'all." Sue smiled at the chefs and the attentive woman. "*Gracias* for being so nice."

"*Grazie,*" the chef instructed her. "*Italiano* for 'thank you' is *grazie.*"

"*Grawts-ee,*" Sue repeated, first to the young man and then to the woman. The chefs grinned and exchanged glances. I wondered if Sue had any idea how undeniable her Texas accent was or what a rarity she must be with her remarkable red hair.

The vaporetto came to a stop. Sue and I stepped off the boat, following several other pedestrians down an alley, and entered a broad thoroughfare. I pulled out a copy of the e-mail that had the directions to where Sue and I were to meet Steph, the woman who had the keys to our apartment.

"If this is *Strada Nuova,*" I said, "then we should go right and watch for *Campo Apostoli.*"

"Campo Apostoli is a restaurant, right? Or you said maybe it's a hotel."

"I'm not sure. The directions just list Campo Apostoli, as if it will be obvious when we see it. Let's head this way and find out."

Sue hesitated.

"It's okay; don't worry. I have Steph's mobile phone number if we get lost."

"Do you know how to use an Italian pay phone?"

"Probably. I don't know. We'll find out. Come on." I picked up the pace, challenging Sue to keep up.

A surprising number of pedestrians passed us. I wouldn't have expected so many people to be out early Sunday morning. Some of the strolling people were dressed in casual attire, but most were in nice outfits—"Sunday-go-to-meetin'-clothes" as some of our friends in Dallas would say.

"Did you notice how you and I are the only people on the thoroughfare with luggage?" Sue asked.

"Are we? Well, I don't imagine we'll see a lot of other tourists since the place we're staying is in a residential area."

"How did these friends of yours find this place?"

"I don't know. They have their annual strategy retreat in a different place each year, so it's possible this is their first time in Venice."

"I hope we find more people who speak English."

"I have an Italian phrase book if we get stuck. Don't worry, Sue. We'll find our way."

Sue didn't look convinced. At that point, I was feeling comfortable enough for both of us. Energized, actually. Venice was new to me yet somehow sweetly, faintly familiar. I felt as if a part of me that had been hibernating for decades was awakening and beckoning me to open my eyes wide to all that was around me.

We approached an open area—a piazza—and headed for the shade of a scruffy-looking tree with a generous canopy of leaves. It was the first tree I recalled seeing so far. I smiled at the brave tree, imagining how it must have sprung from the uneven cobblestones hundreds of years ago, and the inhabitants had celebrated the fledgling by declaring a ban on building within a modest fifty-yard radius of the welcome intruder. It was a protected tree. Rare and honored. And all who gathered under the shade of its branches must surely appreciate it for its singularity.

Sue pointed to a café on the corner. "Do you suppose that's it? Is that *Camp-o Apo*—whatever it was?"

The curved letters painted on the outside of the storefront read "Paolo's."

"No, I don't think so." I looked around. The walkways radiated from this hub in four different directions.

"Maybe he knows where we can find Campo Apostoli." I nodded toward a gentleman in a dark suit. He was seated on one of the park benches beneath the tree's shade, reading a newspaper.

"Are you actually thinking of going over there to ask him, Jenna?"

"Actually, I was thinking you should go ask him."

"Me?"

"Yes, you."

Moistening her lips, she looked at me and in a low voice said, "I asked you for this, didn't I? When you invited me to come, I said I would join you in this insane undertaking as long as you agreed to throw me in the deep end, and that's what you're doing, isn't it?"

I nodded. "You can do this, you know."

She drew in a deep breath. "We'll find out, now, won't we?"

With her determined chin leading the way, Sue took small steps toward the stranger. I followed close behind, thinking how much I admired my brother's wife. She was a strong, courageous, and underestimated woman. I was thrilled when she had caught a glimpse of those qualities in herself and, without my prompting, had made the "deep end" request before we had left home.

I figured this was my first chance to make good on that promise.

"Excuse me, sir," Sue said, and the man lifted his eyes to study us. She spoke slowly and loudly, as if he could understand her better if she treated him as someone who

was hard of hearing. "Do you know where we might find a place called Camp-o A-po-stal-ee?"

He looked at Sue as if she were a strange little red-feathered bird that had landed on the cobblestones before him and now stood there helplessly peeping with her head cocked.

Reaching for the e-mail in my hand, Sue pointed to the words and stated, "Camp-o A-po-stal-ee."

An expression of recognition on the man's face was followed by a nod. "*Qui,*" he said, pointing to the bench and making a circle with his finger around the small plaza area.

"*Kwee?*" Sue repeated his single, definitive word.

"*Si.* Qui. Campo Apostoli. Qui."

"This is Campo Apostoli?" I asked, putting together the pieces. "This little park is Campo Apostoli?"

Now he was the one tilting his head and looking at me like a curious bird. "Si," he said. "Qui. Campo Apostoli."

"Oh, of course," I said. "I remember now. A *campo* is like a plaza. This must be it then."

Giving him her sweetest smile, Sue tried out her first Italian word. "Grawt-see."

He gave her a grimaced response.

"It's my accent, isn't it?"

I nodded. She tried again. "Grat-see."

The man held up his hand with all his fingers pinched together at the tips and touched the edge of his lips. He spoke in slow, exaggerated Italian and measured out the word, "Gra-tsye," effortlessly, putting a spin on his "r." Again he repeated the word with the accent on the first syllable and continued to expressively use his hand. "Gra-tsye."

Sue tried again, this time involving her hand in the process, as if she were trying to pluck the word from the edge of her lips. "Graw-tsye."

The man turned to me, as if we were students in his open-air classroom, and it was my turn to recite the morning lesson. He didn't know that my Midwest background, along with my fascination with accents, would make this an easier task for me than for Sue.

"Grazie." I found the word carried a familiar feeling on my tongue, even though it had been ages since I'd last tried it.

"*Bella!*" he declared with a clap of his hands.

"You little show-off!" Sue teased.

A loud clanging sound echoed from Paolo's café in the corner of the piazza. We turned to watch as a stocky man in a white shirt rolled up a metal awning. He then went to work, removing chairs that had been stacked during the night and placing them around the outdoor tables.

"Looks like the café is opening. Do you want to wait over there? We can sit at a table and order some breakfast," I suggested.

Sue nodded, and I said "*ciao*" to our gracious teacher.

He repeated a long sentence in Italian that I hoped was polite.

"What does '*chow*' mean?" Sue asked. "I've heard that before."

"'Hello,' 'good-bye,' 'see you later.'"

"You really should do all the conversing, Jenna."

"Why? Because I can say *grazie* and *ciao*? Those are the only words I know."

"And *camp-o*. That's three times as many as I know. And people here understand you. They just look at me like I'm the most pitiful thing they've seen in a month of Sundays."

"No they don't."

I stepped up to the counter of the open café. In front of us was a freezer and under the frosted dome were several shallow metal bins of something that I felt happy to see after all these years. Gelato. Rich, creamy, dense Italian ice cream.

"Buon giorno," the man in the white shirt greeted us.

"Buon giorno," I repeated. "Two gelato?" I held up two fingers like a peace sign.

"*Due,*" he said, instructing me by holding up his thumb and forefinger and pointing them to the side like a gun. I remembered then how Italians counted, always starting with their thumb as "one."

"*Si, due gelato, per favore.*" I turned to Sue. "What flavor do you want?"

"What do you mean, 'flavor'? What are you doing? You're carrying on now in full sentences. I'm lost."

"Oh. Sorry. Gelato. Italian ice cream. The world's best ice cream, to be precise."

"For breakfast?"

"Sure, why not? We're on vacation. We can eat ice cream for breakfast, lunch, and dinner, if we want."

"Okay," Sue said slowly. I realized how quickly I could take charge. I had promised Sue I wouldn't overpower her on this trip. Being a single mom for so many years had placed me in the role of the designated leader almost every day. I was entering a new season of life; it was time to pull back. Relax.

"Would you like ice cream or something else?" I asked Sue.

"No, ice cream is fine. It's milk, right? I'll tell myself it's a breakfast drink, only frozen."

"What flavor do you want?"

"I don't know. What flavors do they have?"

I knew I didn't want to try this man's patience so I suggested chocolate.

"*Cioccolato?*" he said, going to work with the metal scooping paddle in his hand, sliding the server into the creamy chocolate.

"*Chalk-o-lot-o?*" Sue repeated. "Well, I'm happy to know that the word 'chocolate' is so similar in our two languages. That could be the only word I manage to remember all week!"

"Then it's a good thing it's one of the more essential

words." I reached for several euros to pay the waiter. "And sorry about running ahead of you there. You will let me know when I'm getting too bossy, won't you?"

"Jenna, that wasn't bossy. Don't worry; I'll let know you when you're bossy. Not that I think you will be. I just didn't realize you were going to start carrying on in complete Italian paragraphs with every man we met within our first hour in Venice. You move fast, girl!"

I laughed, and Sue gave me "the smile." The one with which she looks directly at me with her warm, brown eyes, and everything about her expression and posture says, "We're sisters. Sisters by marriage. Sisters of the heart. Sisters in a spirit of irrevocable bonding. That's not going to change. Not now. Not ever. But even if we weren't sisters, I'd still like you. I'd still want to be your friend."

I held my cup of chocolate gelato and fought back an urge to give way to a flood of tears.

I know. How pathetic, right? Crying over frozen milk. Actually, even though I'm sure a touch of jet lag was involved, I think the real reason I wanted to cry was because of the way Sue accepted me just the way I was. That had not always been the case. We had experienced a long history of family disconnection, which is why I still found her acceptance of me so startling. Every time she looked at me like that I felt I was being offered a tender gift in the second season of life. And for every woman, but especially, I think, for single moms, friendship is such a welcome gift.

"*Chock-o-lat-o*," Sue repeated as she headed for one of the outdoor tables. "I have to remember that word."

"You will," I said, pulling myself together. "You'll remember this." The comment might have been more for me than for Sue. I had a feeling I would remember this morning for the rest of my life.

Two

*P*arking *my* *luggage* beside one of the outdoor tables of Paolo's café, I sat down and watched Sue take her first taste of gelato.

Her eyes opened wide. She sat up straight and looked at me as if I had just fulfilled some long-forgotten secret wish of hers.

"Sweet peaches, Jenna! You weren't kidding about this being the world's best ice cream." She went for another taste. "What do they put in this stuff? It's fabulous."

"I know." I let another spoonful melt on my tongue. "It has something to do with how they make gelato in small batches with milk instead of cream and how the process doesn't use a lot of air."

"I think I have a new project," Sue said. This declaration coming from the scrapbook queen was not surprising.

The only surprise was that the announcement arrived earlier in the trip than I would have expected. But then, she had been looking for something to organize since she knew I was an unreliable subject.

"What's your new project?"

"I'm going to try every flavor of Italian gelato at least once while we're here."

"Excellent project. Will you be needing an assistant?"

"You know it! How many flavors did you see in the freezer here? Six? Maybe eight? I think we should try a new flavor every day. Every morning, if we wanted!" Sue laughed at the whimsy of her goal.

"You know this isn't the only gelato stand in Venice," I said, expanding her vision. "And not all of them have the same flavors. Soon you are going to find out that you're a woman with many gelato options in Italy."

Sue shrugged with cunning. "I've never been one to turn away from a challenge. You know that. Remember, this trip is all about jumping into the deep end. If testing all the gelato in Venice requires that I work morning, noon, and night, well, so be it."

"So be it," I agreed.

We finished our gelato, exchanging only happy "mmm's" and knowing nods.

I leaned back, drew in a deep breath, and exhaled slowly. The morning air felt cool and calming and was tinged with the faintest scent of fresh coffee brewing somewhere nearby. Church bells chimed the glad hour, calling the faithful to worship.

"When is Steph supposed to meet us?" Sue asked.

"Nine-thirty."

"And what time do the men arrive?"

"Not until tonight. Around six. You saw the final e-mail with the schedule, didn't you?"

"Yes, but…"

"We can relax, Sue. We have all day to get organized."

"I don't know if I remember how to relax."

"Would another round of gelato help?"

Sue laughed. "Maybe later."

We settled back, watching the foot traffic move down the Strada Nuova. The thoroughfare hummed with Sabbath comers and goers. Two older women strolled past our table, leisurely walking arm in arm, possibly on their way to or from church. Both wore flattering skirts that skimmed the top of their knees. They had on silky blouses that caught the morning breeze and billowed around the shoulders. Slim-styled leather shoes covered their tanned feet. Classy women.

One of the shop owners stepped outside his door and called out something to the women. They turned to greet him. He leaned against the side of the building, looking like a forty-five-year-old rebel without a cause. A motorcycle might have helped accessorize his missing cause, but motorized vehicles weren't allowed on these streets. Two girls came skipping in our direction. They looked to be about eight or nine and could have been twins. Both were dressed in black-and-white striped, knit dresses and both wore their dark hair up in bobbing ponytails. Arms linked, they skipped in unison, giggling at some shared secret.

Oblivious to us, our luggage, and our curious gazes, the young innocents entered Paolo's. Emerging a moment later, they worked together to open a packet of gum and judiciously tore the first stick in half to share it.

Sue nodded in their direction. "Aren't they the cutest? Sisters, I'm guessing. Sunday treats all around."

She sighed, as if beginning to relax for the first time since she had left her house. "This is really something, Jenna. I keep wondering when I'm going to wake up."

"It's not a dream. You're really in Venice."

Sue looked down as a tiptoeing pigeon patrolled the ground around our table in search of morning crumbs. Without a word, she closed her eyes and drew in a deep breath. The usual concern crinkles that ran in dipped lines across her forehead vanished.

"It's good to see you like this," I told her.

"See me like what?" She opened her eyes and touched the side of her mouth. "Do I have chocolate on my face?"

"No, you don't have chocolate on your face. You look like goodness and mercy are hot on your trail."

Sue gave me a peculiar look. "Goodness and mercy?"

I didn't know what had sparked the image of invisible

goodness and untouchable mercy. Was it the skipping sisters? Sue playfully looked behind her chair. "I don't see them. Maybe they're following you."

"I certainly hope so." The constant flow of pedestrians and the absence of wheels and engines were becoming more noticeable as another wave of church bells filled the air with their resonating chimes.

Another woman walking toward the café caught our waiter's eye, and he called out a greeting. The slim young woman wore sunglasses and had her blond hair twisted up in a clip with one long strand trailing over her shoulder in an artful curve. She stopped to chat with our waiter, leaning forward so he could make a kissing gesture on her right cheek and then her left. He continued to talk during the effortless greeting.

The two of them spoke for a few moments, he nodded, and then the young woman strode in our direction, looking at us inquisitively.

"Buon giorno." Her greeting was calm and direct. "Are you Jenna?"

"Yes. You must be Steph."

"I am. How was your flight?"

"Great. This is Sue."

The three of us shook hands politely.

"It's nice to meet you," Steph said.

Sue spoke slowly, as if trying to make sure Steph understood her. "We-are-glad-you-speak-English."

When Steph didn't respond right away, Sue added, "Your-English-is-very-good."

Steph removed her sunglasses with a bemused expression on her face. "Thanks. I'm from Kansas. I was raised on the stuff."

"Oh! I thought you lived here."

"I do. I'm a student." Steph casually pulled up a chair and gave us a few more details about the overseas study program she was participating in and about her uncle who owned the apartment and had hired her to handle the rentals for English-speaking guests.

Our attentive waiter delivered a demure cup of dark coffee for Steph. On the side of the cup's saucer were two uneven cubes of raw sugar.

"Would either of you care for a cappuccino?" Steph asked. "Paolo here makes the best cappuccinos on this side. This is one of my favorite morning stops."

"Sure," we agreed.

Steph held up her thumb and forefinger the way I'd seen Paolo do earlier as she ordered two cappuccinos for us in Italian.

He responded to Steph, speaking in Italian but all the while looking at us with a grin.

"He wants to know if you would like some more gelato to go with the cappuccinos."

Sue and I exchanged sheepish expressions and shook our heads. Our breakfast secret had been discovered.

Steph said something to Paolo in Italian and then turned her head as he walked away and called back a response to her over his shoulder.

"I hope you don't mind being treated like Italian women now." Steph's mischievous eyes reflected how much she loved her life in Italy. "I told Paolo you're going to be here for a while and that you're not just one-day tourists passing through. He'll watch for you. Every time you stop here for a gelato or cappuccino, he's going to flirt with you. It's tradition. Makes older Italian men feel young, I think."

I didn't know about Sue, but Paolo's cultural expressions already were making me feel a little younger, although I wasn't quick to admit that to beautiful, young Steph. One day, years from now, she would know what I was feeling. For now it was gracious of her to spread her canopy of youthfulness so that it covered Sue and me. "So, what flavor gelato did you two have this morning?"

"Chocolate."

"Always a good choice. Next time try the *stracciatella al caffe* if you like coffee with chunks of chocolate. Or try the *fior di latte*. Very creamy. Oh, or *panna cotta*. That's my all-time favorite. Unless you prefer fruit. In that case, the *sorbettos* are pretty amazing. Try the *limoncello* or the Bellini peach."

"Wait, wait, wait," Sue said, going for a pen in her bag. "I have to write this down."

Steph laughed. "Are you serious?"

"It's research," Sue said with a straight face. She opened to the first page of the simple, small spiral notebook and suddenly started to cry.

"Sue, what's wrong?"

"The pages are blank," she said in a tight voice.

I gave Steph an apologetic look. I had no idea what my companion was talking about.

"I'm sorry." Sue sniffed back the few tears that had escaped. "It's just that I have another notebook like this at home. That notebook is filled with doctors' numbers, pharmacy hours, and all of my relatives' cell phone numbers. This notebook is new. It's blank. It just hit me that I'm about to make a fresh start."

"And you're using the first page to list gelato flavors," I reminded her. "How's that for evidence of goodness and mercy?"

Sue handed the notebook to Steph. "Could you write down those flavors you mentioned?"

"Okay."

"She likes details," I explained.

"Not a problem." Steph grinned. "My mom is exactly the same way. If she doesn't write things down, she forgets everything. She even has a notepad by the phone to take notes during conversations."

Suddenly I felt small again. For a few glorious hours that morning I'd felt young and free, as if the world were my oyster. (Whatever that saying means.) We were riding vaporettos with young Italian chefs, eating ice cream for breakfast, and being set up by lovely Steph for future flirting.

Then, boom! There it was. The striking reminder that Sue and I were old enough to be this young woman's mother. While Sue might have been having a hard time realizing where she was, I think I was having a hard time remembering how old I was.

Seemingly unfazed by the "like my mom" comment, Sue explained to Steph, "I'm doing an independent study of all the gelato in Venice."

"*All* the gelato in Venezia? That's quite an undertaking."

"I realize that. It's grueling work, but I'm dedicated to my research, and I will see this project through to its conclusion."

"Plus she has an assistant," I added brightly.

Steph looked at us as if trying to decide if we were playing a joke on her. A smile grew on her rosy lips. "You two are hilarious."

"No," I said. "You don't know my sister-in-law. She's serious about this."

Steph laughed and then leaned forward, as if we were best friends sharing confessions over our coffee. "I have to tell you something. When I first heard the renters were two women over fifty, no offense, but I didn't expect two women like you."

"What did you expect?" I wanted to know.

"Well, you know. Older women. Over fifty. Gray-haired ladies like my mom." She hesitated and added, "I thought I'd have to carry your luggage for you and do your grocery shopping. But you two are nothing like my mom. She never could make a trip like this. You two rock! You're definitely a couple of Sisterchicks."

The term was new to us, but Sue and I exchanged favorable glances and embraced the title. I hoped the word carried the connotation that we were women who were younger on the inside than we appeared to be on the outside.

Paolo approached with our perfectly frothed cappuccinos. We leaned back in our patio chairs and leisurely sipped the satisfying brew.

"This is nice," I said. I mostly was referring to the leisurely pace of the morning and the way we were able to sit enjoying conversation with this young American woman. Steph must have thought I was referring to the cappuccino.

"I'll warn you now," she said. "It will be difficult to go home and try to find coffee like this. The Italians treat their barista skills as a serious art form. You probably already know this, since so many of the coffee terms in the U.S. are in Italian, but 'espresso' is an Italian term."

Sue and I nodded, but honestly, I hadn't paid much attention before. Although I did love ordering a caramel *macchiato* every now and then, just so I could say the lilting word aloud. Especially if I decided to have the *venti* size.

"Are you ready for me to try to impress you with my Italian?" Steph asked.

"Of course we are," Sue said sweetly.

"*Espresso* comes from the phrase, *espressamente preparato per chi lo richiede,* and that means, 'expressly prepared for the one who requests it.' Paolo holds to that tradition. Each cup is made expressly for you. It's an Italian hospitality thing."

"It's a wonderful hospitality thing." I returned to my cup for another sip.

Across from the café, a young man stepped into the shade of one of the four-story buildings and opened a violin case. He tuned up and began to play out in the open, as if this were a great concert hall and today was first audition. We were the only audience sitting and listening.

"How beautiful," I murmured.

"Vivaldi. *Four Seasons.*" Sue hummed along with the tune that was only slightly familiar to me. "He's very good. And look at him, just standing out there in the middle of the street, playing his heart out. You would never see something like that where we live."

"You'll see musicians everywhere in Venezia," Steph said. "And you'll hear a lot of Vivaldi while you're here. Vivaldi lived in Venezia, you know. Venetians love to perform his work. Make sure you go to San Marco at least one night while you're here. My favorite orchestra is at the Florian, but all of them are good. You'll be charged a lot just to sit and listen, but that's part of being in Venezia, right?"

I wasn't sure what Steph was talking about, but I was sure that Sue's tour book would explain what the Florian was and why we should go listen to the orchestra playing there.

Steph pulled a few coins from her purse, and Sue and I did the same. We managed to come up with enough euros to cover the bill Paolo had left on the table.

"What about the tip?" Sue asked.

Steph brushed off the notion. "You can round up the total if you like. Locals don't tip at the small cafés and *trattorias*. Only tourists."

"At the cafés and what?" Sue asked.

"Trattorias. They're the small lunch places. They look like bars and have simple menus with sandwiches and some pasta dishes. Some are called *osterias*."

Sue gave Steph a confused look.

"You'll figure it out. There are lots of places to eat here. All you have to remember is that if you want to be treated like a local, don't leave a big tip at a small place like this. It's practically an insult. You can tip at the nicer restaurants if you want, but the service fee usually is included."

"That's a change from home," Sue said.

"A lot of the men here who work as waiters do this as a

career choice. They're not working their way through school. This is their dream job. They love to serve and to socialize. Paolo, for instance, is the fourth-generation owner of this café. His great-grandfather, also named Paolo, started the café more than a hundred years ago. And most Venetians would consider this a 'new' café. Venezia is a tight, traditional community. They still see themselves as pretty independent from the rest of Italy."

We all called out our farewells to Paolo. He blew a kiss at us. Well, I'm sure the kiss was aimed at Steph, but it still was nice to be next to her when the kiss came her direction.

Steph pretended to ignore the attention and led us across the Campo Apostoli in the opposite direction from the lone violinist. Her skirt swished with each step she took down an alleyway in her clicking, low-heeled sandals. Sue and I trotted behind, coaxing our wheeled luggage over the uneven pavement and trying to prove that for a couple of "mature" women, we still rocked. Well, rocked according to Steph's definition and not rocked as in about to trip and fall on our faces.

I glanced at Sue as she tried to keep up. Both of us seemed determined to prove we had whatever it took to be Sisterchicks.

Three

S teph *walked down one alley*, then another, then turned and led us past a small sidewalk café with green umbrellas and planters spilling fragrant white alyssum over the edge.

"They have a pretty good breakfast," she said. "When they're open. It's a neighborhood café, so that means they don't always adhere to set hours."

"This is the nearest grocery market," Steph said, as we rumbled past a closed-up building that looked like any other old building on that street.

"Are they open whenever they want to be, too?" I asked.

"No, the market has more normal hours. I don't know if this one closes during the afternoon or not."

"Sounds like they take a siesta," Sue said.

"That's right. Venetians shut down everything in the

heat of the day. They go home for lunch and a nap and then open again in the cooler part of the evening. At least that's how it is in the summer. Things change a little when it gets cold."

"How cold does it get?" By my guess the temperature already was in the low eighties, and it wasn't even eleven in the morning.

"Very cold. It snowed last winter off and on for two days. The rains are what make a mess of everything, though. When the canals flood, the only way to get around by foot is on raised wooden walkways that really make me nervous. But it shouldn't rain much while you're here. At least not pour the way it does in the spring."

"What about grocery shopping on Sunday?" Sue asked.

"Closed. Almost all local vendors close on the Sabbath. They'll be open tomorrow."

Sue gave me a sideways glance as we toted our luggage over a wide footbridge. "We could have a problem finding food for the group before they arrive tonight."

"I hadn't thought about that."

"Take them out to dinner," Steph suggested. "The restaurants are open on Sundays. I really like a place not far from the apartment that's on the water. They have great calamari. I'll make a map for you."

Sue and I had slowed our pace considerably. Having given up trying to roll our battered luggage over the footbridge, we lifted the heavy beasts by their top handles.

"How much farther is it?" I tried to catch up and not sound as winded as I was feeling.

Steph stopped on the other side of the bridge. A young man in a rowboat in the canal we had just walked over called out to her. She ignored him. "This is your street. *Ca'Zen.* The apartment you're renting is to the left in the middle of the palace."

I put down my suitcase and noticed Sue scowled when Steph used the term "palace." Nothing appeared palatial about the outward appearance of our accommodations. The only bright feature was the balcony that overlooked the canal. But the balcony looked wide enough to fit only a chair. Maybe two chairs. I figured if we could just sit outside and gaze up and down the canal at the other balconies brimming with flowers and watch the world of Venezia float by on the placid water, it wouldn't matter how medieval the quarters were inside. We could use our imaginations and pretend it was a palace.

At least that's what I thought until I saw what was inside.

Steph stopped in front of a large, double wooden door. "I guess I should justify my comment about this being a palace."

Sue gave me a raised-eyebrow look.

"Only the home of the Doge—the ruler of Venice— could be called a palace. All the other mansions were known as a *Ca'*. So this is Ca'Zen. But I call it a palace."

Sue continued to look dubious as Steph inserted a long metal key and jiggled it in the keyhole.

"You have to be persuasive with this key sometimes. Come on, *bambino*. Open for me. Here we go." Steph pushed the door inward, and we stepped into darkness. The flooring felt like uneven dirt as we found our footing and pulled our suitcases in behind us.

"The light is here," she said with a snap that illuminated our surroundings. The large dirt floor area was empty. It felt like a stall for horses, only no horses plodded the narrow streets of Venice, as they once had long, long ago.

"When you come in, if the light doesn't turn on automatically, you have to come over to this wall to turn it on. This is the only switch."

I glanced at Sue and wondered how she was doing with all this. She had relaxed at the café, but if our accommodations turned out to be as dilapidated on the inside as this unluxurious entrance, I didn't know how she would take it. I had stayed in some pretty primitive locations in my younger days, so this place didn't frighten me—even with the dirt floors, cracked walls, and a game of blind-man's bluff to find the stairs if the lights didn't turn on.

"Don't worry," Steph added. "The lights usually work. All the other people in this building are pretty understanding if you can't get the key to work or if you need assistance. None of them speaks English, but they're all nice people. Watch the first step here. It's unusually high."

"It's marble." Sue stared at where her feet had landed on the first few steps.

"Yes," Steph said without stopping her ascent. "The place is filled with marble. All the floors, countertops, even the kitchen sink. I hope you like marble."

Sue looked as if she were trying to catch her breath. I guessed the shock of so much marble had caught her off guard. When she and Jack moved to a one-story house a few years ago, the kitchen had to be remodeled to accommodate his wheelchair. Sue had dreamed of using marble on one of the smallest counter spaces, but they couldn't afford to stretch the budget that far. Here, the luminous Italian marble was so plentiful we were walking on it. Walking up three flights of marble stairs.

I was out of breath when we reached the top. I set down my luggage and leaned against the wall.

"You okay?" Steph asked both of us.

I nodded and forced a smile. Sue wheezed a breathless, "Great!" Neither of us was willing to give Steph any reason to lump us into the category of incapable, as she had with her "gray-haired" mother.

Steph showed us two more keys as we stood by the front door. "You need both of these because the door has multiple locks. Open the top one first. Like this."

Sue and I watched and nodded. The door opened inward, and as it did, we gawked at the ornately decorated, spacious room and didn't move.

"Sweet peaches!" Sue exclaimed.

"Are you sure you didn't just break into a back door to a museum?" I asked.

Steph chuckled. "No, this is the apartment. Most of the furniture was replaced in the late 1700s and early 1800s, and of course all the light fixtures are from the early 1900s. Some of the marble floors are original. This is the entry room."

"Don't you mean the dining room?" Sue touched the thick, highly polished dining room table that dominated the center of the room with eight ornate, high-back chairs tucked into their proper places. Two of the walls had glass-fronted bookcases while framed pen and ink drawings of scenes from the Old Testament hung from the other wall. Even with the commanding table in the center, plenty of space remained to navigate the entry room with our suitcases.

"No, there's a separate dining room. But first come through this way to the sitting room."

Steph led us into a magnificent room, as grand as any palatial parlor from castles I'd visited years ago in Germany and Austria.

"Are you sure this is where we're staying? I mean, are you certain this is the rental apartment?" I asked.

Steph nodded. "This is Venezia. It's like this everywhere. Too much, isn't it?"

"It's amazing."

The sitting room was large enough to seat twenty people with space left for another twenty to stand. The beautiful, inlaid mosaic design on the marble floors was mesmerizing. On two of the walls a life-size fresco filled the area with noble grandeur. The left wall was covered with a faded tapestry that I'm sure had a detailed story all its own. The wall directly ahead of us was framed with three windows that had to be ten feet high and came complete with billowing sheer drapes.

"Look at the ceiling," Sue murmured, head back, gaze fixed on the decorative trim and the painting of a serene blue sky and fluffed-up clouds where three floating cherubs reached for each other with pudgy hands. "Who painted this?"

"Who knows?" Steph said with a shrug. "I'd guess it was one of the many greats who turned Venetian homes into their private art schools. The dining room is this way."

Sue and I didn't move. We were still captivated by the beautiful ceiling.

"It's like the Sistine Chapel," I said.

Steph chuckled over her shoulder. "Not exactly. It's nice, but you'll soon see so much of this kind of Byzantine and Romanesque art that it'll all start to look the same." Motioning to one of the three couches in the room, she said, "That sofa with all the old silk pillows covering it is the most comfortable for sleeping."

I did a quick count of the luxurious chairs and couches

in the room. Eleven. And three small, square tables set up like our version of game tables or card tables. Only nothing was "folding" about these tables with their carved wooden pedestals and inlaid wood tops.

Sue and I drew close as we headed for the dining room. "Did you have any idea this place was so extravagant?" she asked.

"None at all. I thought it would be an old building, but since it was 'restored,' I assumed it would be a modern apartment inside with chrome appliances and plastic dishes like the time-share condo my parents used to go to in Aspen."

As soon as we stepped into the dining room, I knew we wouldn't be dining on plastic dishes. Two ornate china cabinets offered us the finest in stemware, china, and crystal carafes. Another solid table with carved legs and six matching chairs sat under the most amazing glass light fixture I'd ever seen. The long plumes of glass fanned from the top of the chandelier like elegant ostrich feathers. The perfectly balanced glass holders for the five light bulbs that rested under the fanned-out plumes transformed the center of the room into a carnival of light the same way a spewing fountain in the center of a town plaza brings life. Above the radiant light fixture the painted ceiling portrayed another scene of floating angel babies. Built into the front wall, between two more ten-foot windows, sat a stately working fireplace with a marble mantle. "I feel like I have to sit down." Sue steadied herself by grasping the back of a chair as she stared at the high ceiling.

Steph glanced around as if trying to see what Sue saw. "The floor is uneven under the table so be careful when you walk around the backside. It shouldn't be a problem, but just know that it's permanently sloped due to the building's settling. Are you ready to see the kitchen and bedrooms?"

"Do you want to wait here?" I asked Sue.

"No, I'm ready. I've just never seen anything like this in my life. I can't believe we get to stay here."

As if a breather for our senses, the kitchen was mild. No painting by undiscovered masters appeared on the ceiling or walls. Everything was simple. Sue couldn't stop running her hand over the marble top of the kitchen table. The table was rectangular and large enough to fit six chairs around it comfortably.

"Do y'all know how much this grade of marble goes for in the U.S.?" Sue asked. "I mean, even a cutting-board size of this sort of marble. This is incredible."

Steph told Sue to brace herself before she showed her the large sink, also in marble.

To this day I don't think Sue has recovered from the marble overdose. Especially because the marble flooring continued through the rest of the apartment. With Steph at the helm, we floated down the hall.

"This is the linen closet," she said. "You'll have to make up all the beds because our maid service just cleans the towels and sheets, but she doesn't make the beds. Don't ask me why; it's odd, I know. I've asked her before, but she refuses. So now we just tell all the guests they have to make up the beds."

"No problem," I said.

As we continued the tour, I counted five moderate-sized and moderately decorated bedrooms before we viewed two tiny "water closets." Just when I thought we had made a complete circle back to the entry room, Steph opened a side door and invited us into the ultimate princess bedroom.

"This is my favorite room," she said. "I love the pale green color of all the furniture. I call it the 'Beauty and the Beast' room. You know, the video in which all the castle staff have been turned into furniture, and they start to sing and dance when Belle shows up."

I vaguely remembered watching the animated video many years ago. When I looked again at the matronly bureau drawers, I saw what Steph meant. The furniture in this princess bedroom did appear to have some dormant performing skills hidden beneath the pale green paint.

The floor space had to be comparable to the gigantic sitting room we had viewed earlier. At the far end of the magnificent room, double-slatted doors opened to the balcony I'd viewed from the street. Bright afternoon sunlight streamed in when Steph threw open the shuttered doors. Sue gave a happy little sound when she saw the piano.

"Do you play?" Steph gave the keys a playful plunk.

"A little," Sue said modestly.

"She used to teach piano lessons," I said. "All three of her grown children are very accomplished. Her oldest son went to college on a music scholarship."

Sue headed for the piano without adding any details. That's when I remembered they had sold the piano when they moved into the new house. This would be a treat for her to play again.

I checked out the twin beds and matching vanity table, complete with rounded mirror and padded, pullout seat. On the opposite wall was a tall dresser that reminded me of a dress form for a broad, buxom woman.

Sue played a light, airy tune on the piano, and the room filled with an enchanting happiness.

"Lovely," Steph said.

"Keep playing," I urged, lowering myself to the edge of one of the beds. "It's the perfect music for this room. Look at the detail on these headboards and footboards. Hand-painted, no less."

"I know," Steph agreed.

As Sue closed her eyes and let her fingers express her feelings in music, I walked across the room to check out the balcony. My estimations were correct; we could fit a couple of chairs on the balcony, sit in the sun, and soak up the gorgeous view of the canal that ran the length of our street. I would be happy to sit there for hours and watch all the quiet activity of this peaceful neighborhood.

Sue finished the music with a run of high notes fading slowly as she barely touched the keys.

"That was beautiful," I said.

"Good to see someone using that old piano," Steph said. "I hate to break this up, but the last rooms I need to show you are the main bathroom and the storage closet. Are you ready to see them?"

Sue and I completed the tour with an introduction to an elongated bathroom that had a shower attachment inside the tiled tub. It was the most updated part of the apartment since indoor plumbing obviously hadn't been part of the original palace floor plan.

At the end off the hall was the final door Steph opened. "The space under the stairs is where you'll find extra cleaning supplies."

"Where do the stairs lead?" I asked.

"To a small space on the roof. You can take laundry up there if you want to dry it quickly. You saw the washing machine in the kitchen, right? Although in summer your clothes will dry just as quickly indoors once you open the shutters at both ends and let the breeze through. That's the advantage of being on the third floor."

I poked my head into the storage area and tried to see where the stairs led, but all was dark after the first four steps.

"Can you think of any questions? You have my contact information, right? And you understood my instructions earlier about getting the trash down to the street level before eight on Tuesday morning. What have I forgotten? Oh, the name of the restaurant where you can take your group tonight. I'll write that down. And anything you find in the kitchen to eat is yours."

We said ciao to Steph and meandered back into the kitchen to figure out what resources we had available. The refrigerator was small and narrow like most European refrigerators. I checked inside and found a few condiments, some Roma tomatoes still connected to the vine, and two waxed cardboard boxes full of fresh green beans.

Sue opened a cupboard door on the decorated wooden sideboard. "We have pasta. Lotsa pasta. And some olive oil and garlic cloves."

"Good. That means we have enough to eat dinner here. We can do our grocery shopping in the morning nice and early. What should we do next? Take our luggage into the princess suite?"

"Slight problem, Jenna. Did you count beds while we were on our tour?"

"No."

"There are five bedrooms. Each of the five bedrooms has only one bed, except the first one and the princess room."

"Is this a trick question?"

"No, there's nothing tricky about it. We have a total of seven beds."

"Seven beds for seven 'brothers,'" I quipped.

"Right. And no beds for the cooks."

"Oh."

"Yeah. 'Oh.' Where are you and I supposed to sleep?"

"Well..."

"You know what, Jenna? I wonder if that's why Steph pointed out the comfortable couch in the sitting room. She knew two people would need to use those couches as beds."

"Okay, so you and I will sleep on the couches. It's only for the first few nights while the men are here. When they leave, we get the princess suite all to ourselves. What do you think?"

Sue didn't look thrilled.

Just then a breeze skimmed across the marble floors.

"Ahh." I closed my eyes and felt the swirling air across my face. "God is breathing His blessing on us."

Sue pulled up her unruly hair into a bunch with her left hand, letting the coolness of the room minister to her perspiring neck. "You're right," she said slowly. "Just being here is an extravagant blessing. I don't know why the thought of sleeping on the couch got to me the way it did."

"I do."

Sue looked amused. "You do? You know what's going on in my psyche? Tell me."

"You've been sleeping on far too many couches and

chairs in waiting rooms and doctors' offices over the past few years. Sleeping on anything but a bed means 'unsettled' to you. It means you can't really relax. It means you're on duty and that you're out in the open and at any moment someone may wake you, and you'll have to get up and manage more trauma."

Sue twisted her closed lips into the kind of pressed-together scowl she made when she was trying not to cry. "You're right." She let down her hair and sunk into one of the nearby chairs.

"This is a new season for you, Sue. For both of us. Couches can now mean sleepover fun or adventure and happy times. Not all couches are cursed."

Sue nodded slowly. "You're right. New beginnings. A season of refreshing. Isn't that what we decided this trip was going to be for both of us? Jumping into the deep end."

"Yes. New beginnings. Refreshing. And sleeping on couches for a few nights."

"I can do that." She sounded as if she needed a little more convincing. But, as I'd seen her do many times during the past few years, Sue stood and put on her determined face. She could tough her way through any difficult situation. Didn't mean she liked it. But she pushed hard and always got through.

"We should make the beds first," she said with an air of

authority. "Then they'll be ready whenever the guys arrive. After that, why don't you and I go to the restaurant Steph suggested for lunch?"

"Sounds good to me." It struck me that whenever any of us come into unfamiliar situations that feel out of control, our instinct is to try to take control. Sue was doing a pretty good job of finding her place, and if taking control of the schedule helped her to settle in, that was fine with me. Strangely, I didn't feel as if our circumstances were out of control. I felt very much at home. I loved this place. What if I decided I wanted to live here for the rest of my life?

And why couldn't I? What's stopping me?

I think that was the first moment in all my years of singleness that I realized how utterly free I was. I could go anywhere. Do anything. There might even be places in the world where I could live and serve with no one really caring that I was divorced.

A new sense of hope stirred inside me as Sue and I made the beds. If I truly was entering a season of new beginnings, it seemed the first step would be a reshaping of how I viewed the opportunities before me and myself. Was I really bankrupt because of my "limitations"? Or was I rich in options? These were all new thoughts, but each thought planted a seed of hope in my heart.

"I'm not done yet," I said aloud.

Sue gave me a strange look at my offhanded comment. "I know. We have three more beds to make."

I didn't try to explain. Instead, I went about making the rest of the beds as if it were the most important work I'd ever done. I was in training for something, but I didn't know what it was.

Four

I t took Sue and me nearly an hour to make up all the beds and sort out the towels. We placed a folded set of towels on the foot of each bed and organized the kitchen a bit.

A drooping cobweb hung from the high ceiling above the sink, so I went to the storage closet in search of a long-handled broom to knock it down. Once again, the view into the darkness above the stairs inside the closet intrigued me. I felt around on the wall for a light switch but didn't find one. Carefully taking the first three steps up, I came to a small landing where the stairs turned and made an angular ascent into the darkened shadows. If this was where the laundry was carried up to the roof, I imagined the maid of a Venetian nobleman had taken this journey with a basket of washed clothes on one hip and a candle in the other hand.

It was a safe guess that my organized sister-in-law had packed a flashlight, and I had a penlight in my purse. I considered going back down to fetch a light, but the Nancy Drewness of the moment urged me onward. I was on a quest in the darkness.

Four more steps up my eyes began to adjust. Two more steps, and my head bumped against what I thought was the ceiling but turned out to be a door. I found a thick metal latch. The cool metal didn't feel like any sort of closure found in this century. Or maybe even in the last two or three centuries. I tried pulling on it. When that didn't work, I gave it a yank to the right and then to the left.

"Jenna?" Sue's voice sounded far away. I guessed she was still in the kitchen.

"I'm up here, in the broom closet."

I could hear her shoes tapping across the marble floor, coming in my direction. She entered the storage room and in a confused voice asked, "Jenna, are you in here?"

"Up here. Up the stairs."

"In the dark?"

"I'm trying to open the door to the roof Steph told us about."

Sue climbed up the stairs behind me. "I can't see a thing. Where are you?"

"Only another five or six steps."

"I feel like Nancy Drew."

"I do, too!" I said. "Which book was the one about the

creepy old mansion? Was that *The Hidden Staircase*?"

"I don't remember." Sue was on my heels now. "So, where's the door?"

"Here." I tried to lean back to give her space to wedge in beside me. "Can you feel this ancient latch? I can't figure out how to make it open."

Sue reached up, and we worked together in the dark, our hands tangling together, as we tried to figure out the medieval lock. We somehow managed to turn it just the right way and were rewarded with a promising click.

"Should we open it?" Sue said.

"Of course. Come on. On the count of three, push."

Blinding midday sunlight gushed into our narrow cavern and caused us both to look away. Instant heat flooded the cooled space and invited us to take the final steps to the roof. I climbed out onto the sunroof and shielded my eyes from the intense brightness.

"Sweet peaches! Look at this." Sue emerged right behind me. "It's like our own secret hideaway."

The flat area was only about ten feet long and maybe six feet wide. It was level and had drainage holes in the side of the raised wall that was about four feet high and protected the open space on three sides. The fourth side was the elevated extension of the roof that went up another six feet or so and had various odd looking spouts and vents cut into the red tiles.

"I feel like we're on top of the world." Sue's hand

shielded her eyes from the direct sun as she surveyed our surroundings. "This is incredible!"

"It is." We could see over the side of our building into the small square that formed the only open space between our apartment building's backside and the other three buildings. In the center of the cobblestone square stood an old well that had been capped. It was easy to picture life in this small, secluded piazza hundreds of years ago. The women would come to the well while the children tagged along and played games. Their cries and laughter would have echoed off the buildings. I imagined this as a happy corner of Venice.

"Look over there." Sue pointed to the neighboring buildings that also formed a square. "They have trees."

Sue was right. Sprouting up to rooftop level was an immense tree or perhaps several trees that spread their green goodness in a comforting canopy. We'd already seen at Campo Apostoli how rare trees in Venice were and how shade was at a premium.

Straight ahead of where we stood, beyond the rows of red-tiled rooftops and tall, saffron-colored buildings, we could see blue water. In the midday brilliance the blue wasn't the playful aqua I'd seen that morning on the Grand Canal. This blue was deep and brooding. It was the blue of the Venice lagoon where waters from the Adriatic Sea flowed in to greet this fleet of anchored islands. Sue took in the sweeping vista of our quiet neighborhood. "This is amazing."

"It is!"

"I'm having a hard time comprehending how all these buildings, all these huge, intricate structures, have been here for hundreds of years and are built on man-made, or at least man-assisted, islands. The buildings look like a row of dominos, don't they? Take one frontline building, tip it far enough, and the whole row of structures could crumble into the sea."

"I know," I agreed. "It's all so precarious, yet so settled and established. What a strange and wonderful place."

"Well, Nancy Drew, it seems you have another mystery to solve. How does Venice keep from falling into the sea?"

I leaned against the edge of the roof ridge and thought for a moment. "I have no idea. But you know what amazes me, Sue? I was thinking of this earlier today. Or yesterday, I guess, when I was looking out the plane's window. I'm amazed that God holds all of this together. Not only Venice, but also earth. And us. Everything could crumble in a flash if God took His hand off us, if He removed His presence. But He doesn't. He holds everything together."

Sue surveyed the ancient world below us. In a quiet voice she said, "I don't know. Sometimes it feels as though God removes His hand."

I knew she was referring to her husband's car accident.

"You know," Sue continued, "everyone said God had protected Jack and kept him alive and brought him out of the coma after all those months. But my husband is going to spend the rest of his life in a wheelchair."

"I know," I said softly. I had been there every step that took Jack on the journey of recovery over the past two years. My brother's accident was what prompted me to move to Dallas. The hours Sue and I spent together had cemented our friendship. I knew how awful it had all been and in many ways still was.

"So," Sue said, pulling back and folding her arms across her middle, "I'm not sure I'm as convinced as you are that God still holds everything together. God could have stopped that driver from running Jack off the road, but He didn't. I can't explain why God didn't do that."

"Neither can I."

"Jack says it's okay, you know. He says he's accepted it and I should, too. While he watched me pack, he said he was glad I was moving on because that's what he's doing. He's moving on. Adapting." Sue paused, looking out over the rooftops. Her voice lowered as she confessed, "But you know what, Jenna? I don't want to adapt. I want my husband back all the way. I wanted God to be there at the moment of that accident and to hold everything together so Jack wouldn't be hit. That's what I want. But that's never going to happen."

I stood close, listening. For years our conversations had been around the facts, the details, the medical schedules. Sue rarely talked about how she felt. She just took each day as it came.

Not sure what to say or do, I reached over to pat her comfortingly on the shoulder. "It's okay."

Sue pulled away. "No, it's not okay. I'm not okay. Why does everybody keep saying that? My life is not okay, and it's never going to be okay. I will never be able to accept what happened. Not the way Jack has." Sue raised her arms, and in a razor-sharp voice she added, "I am so mad! There, I finally said it. I am so screechin' angry! What happened to my husband wasn't fair. That accident didn't just happen to Jack; it happened to me, too." She thumped her chest with her clenched fist. "That irresponsible driver changed my life, too!"

Backing up a step, Sue leaned against the side wall, as if for support, while the confession continued to leak out. "This isn't the way my life was supposed to go. I never expected something like this. I never prepared for this. Nothing is ever going to be the same."

I wanted to tell Sue how I once felt the way she did now. I once said practically the same words she was saying. I'd never told her about when I hit bottom at the age of thirty-six and was so depressed I didn't think I could go on. That's when I decided to seek out a professional counselor. Once a week I spilled my guts, and by the grace of God and the skill of the counselor, I came around. My perspective changed, and I was able to be honest with myself.

The experience allowed me the chance to come to terms with how emotionally demolished I'd been after the divorce. I remembered feeling each week that I'd made a big mess with a lot of words in the counselor's office. Somehow I felt like I should mop them all up before I left. I wanted Sue to feel she had the freedom to make that big a mess around me now.

Turning to me and taking in my sympathetic expression, she said in a low voice, "I'm sorry, Jenna. I shouldn't have said all that. It just sort of spilled out and…"

Sue was doing exactly what I'd done in my counseling sessions—verbally trying to mop up her words.

"I'm glad you let it out," I said.

"I shouldn't have. You don't need to hear that from me. I didn't realize. It's just… I'm… I'm sorry."

"You don't have to apologize. I know those feelings, Sue."

"Yes, but…"

"Really, Sue, I know those feelings. I didn't expect my life to go the way it did, either."

She tilted her head, as if looking at me through new eyes. "You do know what I'm feeling, don't you?"

"Yes, I do. Different circumstances. Similar feelings. You can say whatever you want to with me anytime."

She drew inward and lowered her eyes. "Thank you, Jenna. But I feel so bad when I let my feelings take over. I shouldn't have…"

"Sue?" I waited till she looked me in the eye. "Shame off you."

She blinked. "What?"

"Don't let even a pinch of shame settle on you. You're doing the right thing by being honest with yourself. I'm a safe person for you to talk to. I understand. There's nothing you need to apologize for. So, shame off you."

The implication settled in like balm on her open wound. All the mama-sister-best friend sympathy that grows large in the heart of a native Texan exploded from Sue. She opened her arms wide and wrapped them around me. We hugged each other as two strong women who had weathered demolishing storms, and yet we were still standing.

"Jenna, Jenna, Jenna, where would I be without you?"

"Well, you wouldn't be in Venice, standing on a rooftop."

"No, I wouldn't. And I wouldn't be clothed and in my right mind, I can tell you that. I would be locked up somewhere in a padded room. Jenna, you've been there for me through all of this. Thank you. Thank you for being strong for me."

I kissed my sis-in-law on top of her fluffed-up red mane. "Suzanne, you're going to make it through all this. You're not going to be carted off to a padded room. You may feel like it some days, but you're a strong woman of great faith and hope."

She managed a hint of a smile. "I don't feel that way."

"That's okay. Feelings aren't everything, you know."

Sue sighed.

We stood side-by-side, gazing out toward the brooding blue water in the distance. Sue leaned her head on my shoulder.

"Shame off me," she whispered, and I smiled. I knew the power those words had held for me many years ago.

We remained like that for a while. Silently holding each other up, feeling the heat of the Italian summer day massage our heads and shoulders, urging us to relax. I decided then that a good recipe for healing any sort of broken heart started with equal parts truth and acceptance. Add the patient understanding of a true friend and then let those ingredients rise under the Italian sun. The results were bound to be delicious.

Five

"Are you hungry?" Sue pulled away from our rooftop shame-off-you session.

"Hungry?"

"I'm hungry. That's a good sign, isn't it? My mother used to say if you would rather eat than weep it means you're feeling better."

"Then let's go eat!"

We made our way down the stairs, changed into cooler clothes, and took the paper with the name of the restaurant Steph had recommended. Sue made sure we had a map and all the house keys, which was a good thing, because my thoughts were on my limited options of cool clothes. I wished I had a flattering skirt to wear like Steph and some of the other women we had seen earlier. Sunday afternoon in Venice just seemed to call for something other than

chinos or jeans. In a supreme effort to pack light, all I'd
brought was one pair of each. I also had packed one
sleeveless blouse, which I wore now to the restaurant.
Shopping was definitely going on my to-do list this week.

Shopping in Venice. I smiled at the thought.

We didn't pass any shops on our way to the
restaurante. We did pass several other restaurants. Each of
them offered outdoor waterfront eating at small tables.
Dozens of afternoon diners were caught up in what we
soon learned was a delight of Venetians: long, luxurious
dining with friends.

Sue and I were shown to a table for two at the water's
edge and were handed small menus.

"This is nice." I took my seat, feeling a warm breeze
rise from the expanse of salty sea.

Sue nodded and used her menu to fan herself. "I
should have worn a short-sleeve shirt like you. Mine all
need to be ironed. This is a different kind of heat than we
have at home. It feels more penetrating and not as humid."

I made agreeing sounds and scanned the menu.
Everything was listed in Italian, but the names were familiar: lasagna, ravioli, and manicotti. This was going to be
easy.

The waiter stepped up and asked something in Italian.

Sue jumped in and said, "Hello. I'd like the lasagna,
por favor. Oh, wait, that's Spanish again. How do y'all say
'please' in Italian? By any chance do you speak English?"

He pinched his thumb and first finger together. "A little."

"Good. I would like the lasagna and sweet tea with lots of ice."

I mentioned to Sue they wouldn't have sweet tea here. They might have hot tea, but iced tea, sweet or otherwise, wasn't a likely beverage to find in Italy.

She looked back at the waiter. "Just a bottle of water then. Lasagna and water with lots of ice."

I ordered the lasagna and water as well. After our waiter stepped away, I tried to explain to Sue why it also wasn't likely she would be served ice with her water. Unless things had changed considerably in European dining since my last visit, ice rarely was served. I told her about one time in Belgium, on a record-breaking summer afternoon, when a friend of mine begged for ice for her drink. The waiter brought a serving bowl with big chunks of icicles to her, as if he had just chipped the frost out of a freezer with a hatchet. After that we learned to adapt to warm soft drinks.

"Guess I have some adjusting to do." She didn't sound thrilled at the thought. "If you don't mind my saying it, Jenna, you didn't tell me how limiting things were going to be here in the deep end."

I leaned in closer. "But you're lovin' it, aren't you?"

"I'm adjusting," she said ambiguously.

A luxurious cruiser boat motored past our restaurant,

carrying what looked like a family, including a dog with his snout to the wind and a grandma who sat in the back, wearing a scarf over her hair. The dad at the helm was using one hand to steer and the other hand to express his feelings to his son, who was standing up and appeared to be arguing with his sister. The boy sat down and folded his arms in disgust. It could have been a Rockwell painting of any family on their way home from vacation, but this family just happened to be going home on a boat instead of in an old Ford station wagon.

Sue looked past all the Sunday afternoon boating traffic. "I wonder if that island over there is the island of Murano. I read about that one in the tour book. It's where they make glass, with the craftsmen demonstrating how glass is blown the ancient way. I'd like to go there if it works out. Oh, wait, I still have the map." Sue pulled it out and pointed to the island across the water from us. "Is that it?"

"*Isola di San Michele,*" I read the words on the map. In parenthesis was the word "*Cimitero.*"

"Cimitero," I repeated and went scrounging for my Italian phrase book. Looking up at Sue, I announced, "That's the cemetery."

"The whole island?"

"I don't know. Possibly. A lot of people have lived in Venice for a lot of years."

"Creepy," Sue said, giving a little shiver. We found Murano on the map and were happy to see that it was just the next island over from the cimitero. We even figured out what vaporetto we could take to Murano and the best time of day to observe the glassblowing.

In the midst of our planning, our waiter arrived with lunch. The water came in a tall plastic bottle with two glasses and no ice. We put away the map and tour book and dove into the lasagna. The meat sauce was flavorful with sausage and herbs and a wonderful balance of light cheese and marinara sauce. I counted seven layers of thin lasagna noodles that were cooked just right. Sue and I both agreed we never had eaten such good lasagna.

"I think I have a new favorite hangout," Sue said, looking around. "Waterfront dining even. Although we still have to put this place to the true test and try some of their gelato."

Sue asked our waiter, in what I thought was a too-loud voice, "What do you think is the best flavor?"

"*Fragole.*"

Sue looked to me for approval or for a translation; I wasn't sure which. I had no idea what fragole was, but I was willing to be surprised, so I gave a supportive nod. Sue ordered "*do-aye fra-goal-ee*" without any idea what we were getting.

The colorful dessert dishes were delivered with a triangular-shaped wafer stuck in the side of a smear of what turned out to be strawberry gelato. I say smear because it looked as if the waiter had taken a small spatula and packed the gelato into the dish rather than scooping it with a rounded spoon.

Sue tried her first taste with an exacting, discerning air. Smacking her lips, she tried a second taste. "Superb. Bright taste. The strawberry flavor comes through clear and sweet without being overpowering."

I laughed. "You're going to turn into a gelato snob, I hope you know."

"There are worse things."

"You know, Sue, I'm wondering if you need to develop a scale system here."

"Why? To see how much I weigh before and after I sample all the gelato?"

"No, you nut. I mean a scale of one to ten to rate your favorite."

"Excellent idea. I give this one a 7.5. No, an 8." She pulled out her notebook. Her unabashed love affair with Italian gelato was in full bloom as she listed her rating.

"What do you rate this *fra-goal-ee* flavor?"

"I'd give it a five."

"Only a five?"

"Okay, a 5.5 but that's my top score. It's nice, but I'm not wild about strawberries."

"You're kidding! I never knew that. What about berries in general? Blueberries?"

I shrugged. "I can take them or leave them. Now, when it comes to apricots…"

"Look it up," Sue said. "Look up the Italian word for 'apricot.' We'll see if they have it."

I flipped through my book and read the word *albicocca*.

Sue made a joke out of the way I pronounced it. "All right, then. You be a Coca Cola and ahl be a Pepsi."

It took me a minute to catch her joke. The waiter approached as I was laughing, and Sue cracked me up even more when she said to him, "Excuse me, sir, but do y'all have *ahl-be-a-coca* ice cream? I mean, gel-ah-toe?"

He looked to me for translation, and in between swallowing my laughter, I formulated the request in a combination of English and Italian and pointed to the word for 'apricot' in my phrase book.

"No." His answer was clear and simple. He walked away.

"Okay, then," Sue said. "We'll just take our gelato business elsewhere. Maybe our Paolo has apricot gelato."

"Do you want to walk back there now to find out?" I asked.

"Are you kidding? I'm ready to walk back to our palace and take a princess-sized nap. Aren't you tired?"

"I could sleep."

With our stomachs satisfied and the heat of the day rising, Sue and I meandered back to our "palace" and worked the key in the front entry. We stumbled our way across the dark, dirt floor and slowly hiked up the three flights of marble stairs. Unlocking the front door took a little more effort with the persnickety locks. But all our work was rewarded when we entered the beautifully cool palace. Instead of winding down the hall to the princess beds, we made a beeline for the two couches in the sitting room. It was the coolest room in the house and immensely inviting.

We didn't even close the shutters to the mid-day brightness. In tandem motion, both of us spread out on the comfortable couches and drifted into our afternoon siestas as if we had been raised on the custom.

The sleep I experienced that day was deep. Deep, restorative, and sweet. I slept for three hours, dead to the world, and woke feeling refreshed.

Sue was still sleeping when I stirred. It looked as if she hadn't moved a muscle from the way she first had lain down. Something impish in me wanted to tiptoe over and find a feather to tickle her nose or her bare feet.

Instead of disturbing her, I studied the frescos on the walls and then turned over and eyed the paintings on the ceiling. The clouds looked light and dimensional, as if they actually puffed out from the ceiling a few inches more than the rest of the painting. I loved the shade of blue in the sky. It was a soft, soothing, reflecting-pool blue and added cool-ness to the room.

From the open windows rose the echoing call of a young child. The voice was so loud that Sue's eyelids fluttered. She turned over and went back to sleep. Rising and going to the open windows as quietly as I could, I looked down on the piazza. The ancient capped well in the center of the cobblestones had become the meeting place for two women and four busy children. Two dark-haired boys wearing shorts and brown leather lace-up shoes with white socks were riding tricycles in circles around the well. Two girls had a rope and were organizing a skipping game, with the taller girl calling out her instructions with universal big-sister authority. Her loud voice had found its way to our quarters and echoed off the high ceilings.

"What time is it?" Sue asked.

"Ten after four."

"You're kidding. Wow, I can't believe how long we slept."

"You have to come see this," I said from where I stood by the window looking down on the piazza. "Look at these children."

The two mothers stood with their arms folded across the front of them, chatting, nodding, and keeping a maternal eye on their little ones. The skipping rope game was in full swing, and the tricycle racers were picking up their speed.

I don't know what Sue was thinking about, but I guessed it was the same thing I was thinking. We were mothers of young children once. And now they are grown. I thought back to when my daughter, Callie, was that young. She was twenty-six now, as independent as all get-out and yet faithful to call me regularly. She had been to Dallas four times to see me in the two years I'd lived there.

Callie and I "grew up" together, just the two of us, tucked into a tiny house in Lake Minnetonka, Minnesota. She and I moved into the cottage when she was five. It had been my grandparents' summer place, and they had left it to me in their will with a request that I never sell it but give it to Callie. I did, and she still lived there with a fat cat named Max and a steady stream of houseguests every summer.

When Callie was seven she asked if she could "paint" her room. She painted a bright yellow sun in the top corner and lined the bottom edge with rows of blue and red posies. From the ceiling she hung five paper butterflies on fishing line that fluttered about whenever the windows were open, welcoming the breeze off the lake. That was apparently the start of her graphic arts career, which was now in full swing at a greeting card company only twenty miles from home.

I remembered all the afternoons Callie and her friends would ride their bikes the four blocks to the lake. I would stand at the front window watching until their bobbing ponytails turned the corner on Mercury Avenue. Callie was an independent thirteen-year-old, and I was a nervous cat. I would make myself busy for an hour or less before I returned to the front window with furniture to dust or laundry to fold while I continued my vigil.

"Women are the same the world over, aren't they?" Sue stood beside me and looked out the window with a tender gaze.

"Yes, we are. And you know what I think? I think what those women are doing right now is a beautiful work of art. Someone should make a tapestry of that or paint a wall with scenes of mothers watching their children play."

"Aren't you poetic! Come on, Jenna. We need to start dinner. Let's see if we can turn our meager supplies into a gastronomical work of art."

"Okay," I said, taking the challenge. "Let's."

Six

That July afternoon, in the Venetian kitchen with the high ceilings that echoed with the voices of gleeful children, Sue and I gathered up the manna left in the pantry and created a work of art in pasta and string beans. What made the experience so beautiful for me was that we were doing this together, in womanly sync, as if it were woven into our DNA. Our movements across the marble floor matched each other's in the steps to this dance.

We were preparing a meal for people we had never met. Of course, I knew Sam, the organizer of the gathering, but I never had met the other men who were coming to this retreat from around the world.

Sue ran through a list of questions while I checked on the boiling water. "You said these men do this retreat every year? Even though they're from different missions?"

"Yes. Sam started the retreat a few years ago to gather these leaders in one place so they would have a chance to form a brotherhood and work in unity with each other."

"It's an excellent concept." Sue rinsed the green beans. "Multiply the efforts by working together instead of as a bunch of individuals." With a wink she added, "It sounds more like something a group of women would have thought of."

I joined her in snapping off the ends of the green beans. They were so fresh we could have eaten them raw.

"This must be quite a journey for some of the men," Sue said. "I wonder where they're all coming from. I hope they get here safely."

I left the room and went to where we had stowed our luggage. I returned with the list of men and the schedule of their retreat.

"Here are their names," I said, going through the list: Peter from India, Eduardo from Argentina, Fikret from Turkey, Bruce from South Africa, Sergei from the Ukraine, Malachi from Kenya, and, of course, Sam.

"Do you know if these guys have a set schedule?" Sue asked.

"I printed out Sam's final e-mail. The schedule is rough. It starts with dinner tonight around six. Afterwards they'll have a meeting."

"In the sitting room, I suppose."

"Possibly."

"You know, Jenna, we're going to have to figure out our sleeping arrangements. If they're in the sitting room every night, where do you and I go when we're ready to sleep?"

"Good question."

"So what's your good answer? I mean, we should figure this out before they arrive. Otherwise you and I are going to be locked in this kitchen until very late every night."

I was beginning to understand the joys and the hidden sacrifices of serving in this way. Hospitality, I decided, was an underestimated gift. Once I heard "hospitality" defined as "showing love to strangers," and it looked as if we were about to experience that definition firsthand. "Let's set the table, and then we can figure out the sleeping problem."

Sue checked on the china plates and glistening crystal glassware in the dining room while I went in search of table linens in the large closet in the hallway. Steph hadn't opened that closet door when she gave us the tour, so I was amazed when I saw that the closet was more like a small room. Against one wall leaned two mattresses.

"Sue, come here!"

She dashed into the closet. "What's wrong?"

"Nothing's wrong. I thought I'd have to yell for you to hear me."

"You don't have to yell. The sound travels in this place."

"Look at these mattresses."

"Yes? So?"

"What if we hauled them up to the roof? We could sleep up there. Or at least use it for our hideaway while the men have their meeting in the sitting room. It will be our tree house!"

Sue looked hesitant. "Do you think it will be okay?"

"I don't see why not. Come on, let's turn off the burners on the food and do this before the guys arrive."

Nothing makes a woman feel old and young at the same time like trying to outfit her improvised tree house by hauling a mattress up a flight of narrow stairs.

Once we managed to heave both mattresses onto the rooftop, I stood back and caught my breath. The evening air swirled with the scent of salt air and garlic. Accordion music floated our way from one of the alleyways where I could picture an aspiring musician playing his or her heart out for locals who were making their evening commute on foot.

Sue went back to the linen closet for sheets while I arranged the mattresses.

High above me the sun blazed its own trail home with less gusto than had accompanied its noonday romp. This steady companion of summer days on the Adriatic Sea willingly bowed to the saucy smile of a moon that had showed up early for work. The quarter moon hung back, diminished in the dusky blue sky, knowing her job was to wait on the slow-moving sun. Her time would come.

"How's it going?" Sue poked her head up through the opening to our rooftop roost.

"Good. I was watching the moon."

Sue joined me with her arms full of linens. "It's beautiful."

Together we went to work, covering the mattresses with the sheets and blankets, and then stood back to admire our Bohemian hideaway.

"We're really going to do this. We're going to sleep outside," Sue said with an eager grin.

"I know. Either we're really crazy or really cool."

"Or both!"

I thought if this didn't prove Sue and I were Sisterchicks, I didn't know what would.

"Do you feel like praying?" I asked.

"Praying?"

I nodded. "We should pray for the men while they're on their way here and pray for our children and—"

"You go ahead. I need to check on things in the kitchen." Sue quickly disappeared down the rabbit hole. I stood alone under the rising moon and offered up my evening prayers.

Praying by myself wasn't uncommon. As a matter of fact, it was familiar. I thought about the way I'd prayed when Gerry walked out. Callie was only a few months old. I had held her and cried and prayed all that night. While I prayed, a thin curl of the new moon rose in the sky, bringing a faint, persistent comfort into the room.

God didn't answer any of my prayers that night the

way I wanted Him to. He didn't give me any of the solutions I begged and bargained for. All God gave me was Himself. His presence. And even though I didn't recognize it at the time, the grace of His presence was sufficient. His abiding Spirit was like the moon. A sliver of comfort and light rising even on the darkest night.

This night, on the Venetian rooftop, His presence was more than sufficient. He filled heaven and earth. He was here. He had never left me. Over all the years, as my circumstances changed, the only constant and unchanging truth was that God was with me.

I stood in awe and whispered, "Thank You." When I returned to the kitchen, Sue said she had everything ready and suggested we place the pasta in the water when the men arrived. She wasn't looking directly at me as she spoke.

"Are you okay?" I asked.

She nodded.

"I wasn't sure, when I asked you to pray and then you left, if that meant—"

"I'm just not where you are in your way of talking to God, okay?"

"Okay."

"I don't want you to push me into the deep end, if you understand what I'm saying."

"I think I do."

"You know how you asked me to tell you if you're

being pushy? Well, just let me, you know, find my place. Get my balance. Everything is coming at me so intensely and…"

I nodded and offered her a comforting smile. "Okay. I understand."

A buzzer sounded, and we looked around.

"Did you set an alarm on the stove?"

"No." Sue looked around the kitchen. "It's not a fire alarm, is it?"

The buzzer sounded again. It stopped and then sounded again, this time longer.

"The doorbell!" we figured out in unison.

"I'll get it." I trotted quickly to the front door. But when I opened it, no one was there. Then I remembered seeing a buzzer system at the wooden door on the street level.

Propping open the front door with a chair, I took the three flights of stairs quickly and entered the dark entryway. The light worked as it was supposed to, and I put my hand to the doorknob, out of breath.

Sam was much older than when I last had seen him. But he still was full of energy. Still young on the inside. His clear eyes smiled at me behind his silver-rimmed glasses. Everything about the man spoke of peace. He had seen much but wasn't afraid.

"Jenna, look at you! Oh, it's good to see you."

"It's great to see you. Come in. Welcome!"

Five men filed in behind Sam, each looking travel

weary but quick to shake my hand. I tried to guess who was who from the list I'd prayed over earlier.

"Did you receive a second set of keys for us when you checked in?" Sam asked.

"Yes, they're on the table in the entry. Wait until you see this place. It's amazing. Sue is up in the apartment, and dinner almost is ready. I'm so glad all of you made it here safely."

"Malachi was delayed on his flight from Kenya," Sam said. "He should arrive later tonight."

"We'll save some dinner for him. What about the rest of you? Would you like to go to your rooms first or eat?"

The men started up the stairs, talking with each other but without answering me.

What followed was a transition into my new role. I realized the implications of being a servant. Vital but nearly invisible. This wasn't my home. These weren't my guests. Sue and I were, in some ways, their guests. We were well-rewarded facilitators hired to serve them.

I felt humbled as I followed the men into the apartment. Each of them selected a room without much discussion. They washed up quickly and took their places around the dining room table. The difference between how men and women generally respond in similar situations was amazing to consider.

I let Sue know they were ready to be served. She and I moved in and out of the dining room, delivering food, refilling crystal goblets, and removing china plates without so much as eye contact from most of the men. One of the men, Peter from India, glanced at me and said the food was good. I quietly apologized to him for the simplicity of the meal, explaining that we hadn't been to the grocery store yet.

Peter assured me the meal was plentiful. I nodded and withdrew to the kitchen where I considered the abundance of food I was around every day. Not only what I ate but also what passed through my hands at the grocery store where I worked.

When the meal was over and all the plates cleared, the men leaned closer over the table and dove deeper into their conversations. Sam looked up as I was removing his plate and asked about the chance of having some coffee or tea.

Sue reported to me in the kitchen that our inventory included only four tea bags. I boiled water in a saucepan, and we let the bags steep for about five minutes. Serving the tea without milk, we placed on the table a china sugar bowl half full of hard sugar lumps. Every man was given a single cup of the stretched tea. On the table we placed a white china teapot filled with the worn-out tea bags float-ing in hot water in case any of the men wanted a second cup. None of them seemed to notice the refills or us.

"It sure is different serving men than serving women," I said once we were back in the kitchen.

"I'm glad they aren't too picky about what we're giving

them," Sue said. "Although I'll sure feel better once we get to the grocery store."

I told her about my thoughts on the abundance of food available to us every day. Then I leaned against the edge of the kitchen sink and kept my voice low. "I could never do this for a living."

"What? Wait on tables? Were you never a waitress?"

"No."

"Well, I worked at a restaurant for two years when I was in high school. I liked the challenge of serving everything while it was hot and providing coffee refills or the check before a customer asked."

I could see how Sue would appreciate such a challenge.

"But I hated seeing so much food being thrown away."

I nodded my agreement.

"What's the plan for breakfast?" Sue asked.

"We'll get up early and go to the bakery so we can serve them a continental breakfast. Sam said they would like to eat at 7:30 each morning."

"What does he mean by a continental breakfast?"

"Just coffee and rolls."

"Do you think the grocery store will be open by then?" Sue asked.

"If not, we'll just go to the bakery and then to the store later."

"This is so different from the way we do things at home."

"I know."

We went back to work side by side, trying to be as quiet as possible in cleaning up the dishes. Once the kitchen was in order, we hung the linen dish towels by the open window to dry. Then we left a note on the table, saying a plate of food awaited Malachi in the fridge if he was hungry when he arrived.

I was more than ready to rest my weary self for the night. I changed into the loungewear I'd packed and consolidated my luggage in a corner of the storage closet. Feeling like a true chambermaid, I turned on my trusty penlight and climbed up the steps to our rooftop sleeping room.

Sue was already on the roof. She turned to me with a serene expression. "Look," she said softly.

At our feet, Venezia had transformed while we were washing dishes. A twilight hush lingered over the darkened water. In every direction we spotted amber lights—lights on boats skimming across the water, lights in windows of homes that lined the piazza, lights tucked in the winding alleys in the distance that promised cafés open for business. With the absence of glaring streetlights, car lights, and other illuminations that brightened the sky in most cities, Venezia took advantage of the flattering glow and showed off what she seemed to consider her best side.

Sue and I looked around for a long time before snuggling into our beds on the rooftop.

Seven

Once Sue and I were tucked cozily into our beds, we noticed that the stars overhead were ready to take over the city's light show, impressing us with their bountiful twinkles.

"I wonder who's sleeping in the princess suite," Sue said.

"Someone who will be as ready as we are for a good night's sleep."

"Do you think we're going to be okay up here?" Sue asked.

"Yes, I think we're well protected." I meant protected by our heavenly Father, but Sue took it to mean protected by the raised wall that kept us out of sight from anyone who might look up in our direction.

"I'd feel more protected if the wall were another foot higher."

"Sue, when was the last time you slept outside?"

She thought awhile. "When I was a Camp Fire Girl. That had to be more than forty years ago."

"Then it's time to sleep once again in the cradle of the night."

Sue responded with a glimmer of the wit that I knew lay just under the surface of her hesitancies. "Do you think we can earn a merit badge for this?"

I chuckled.

"Don't you think it would be nice to have something to show for all we've accomplished in this long day?" she asked, warming up to the topic. "I mean, we flew across the world, for starters."

"And found our way here," I added.

"And set up everything for the men."

"But God clearly provided the food for tonight," I added.

"Yes, but we figured out how everything in the kitchen worked. And we didn't break anything."

"True."

Sue kept going. "You spoke Italian, and people understood you."

"Yes, but you started a fresh page in a new notebook with two, count 'em, due, gelato flavors."

"I did, didn't I? But then, I also bit off all my fingernails today. I don't know if you noticed."

"I noticed."

"Did you really, or are you just saying that?"

"I really noticed. I always notice your hands. I can tell how you're doing by the condition of your fingernails."

"I never knew that."

"There's a lot you and I don't know about each other." Our friendship was formed hard and fast in a time of need. The focus had been on doing all we could for a man we both loved—my brother, her husband. After my divorce I had been ostracized from my family. Callie and I did holidays on our own and for our birthdays didn't expect gifts from family members. In our isolation my darling girl and I became our own family. We did okay, but only because we were part of a wonderful church community that welcomed us as its own.

Everything changed with my family when Jack went into a coma. I showed up, and no one asked where I'd been for twenty years. They just accepted me again, and we all started over. Sue opened her heart to me, and I crawled right in, making a little place for myself as cozy as the birds' nest she and I were settled in now on this Venetian rooftop. She found an equally inviting corner in my heart where she could feel at home.

Sue shifted around in her bed, rearranging the covers.

"Are you comfy?" I asked.

"Getting there."

"Warm enough?"

"Yes." She lay still for a few moments before asking, "Jenna, are you at all nervous?"

"No."

"I don't think I am right now, either. I should be, but I'm not. It's a strange feeling."

"It's a good feeling." I smiled contentedly and soon fell asleep under a canopy of angel winks.

My journey through dreamland was peacefully uninterrupted until the first gleam of light broke over me. With the light came a lot of clatter.

Stretching and crawling out of my blanket haven, I leaned over the left side of our lookout tower, feeling like a spy who peered down on the citizens below. A hand-pushed cart stacked high with boxes that looked like they were on their way to the grocery store came rumbling over the piazza. Without delivery trucks, every item in Venice had to be hand carried, pushed around on carts, or paddled down the canals by boat.

To the right of our turret, a fishing boat with a small outboard motor puttered down the canal. Two well-dressed children sat on the front bench of the boat, swatting at each other.

Sue moaned. "What time is it?"

"Six-thirty."

"In the morning?"

"Yes. Six-thirty in the morning in Venezia, Sue! Buon giorno!"

She rolled over. "Please tell me we don't have to get up yet."

"You don't have to if you don't want to."

"No, I'll get up. See? I'm getting up now." She didn't move.

I stretched and made my bed as best I could.

"How can you be so awake?" she muttered.

"You can keep sleeping, Sue. I can go to the bakery by myself."

"No, I want to go. Really." Still, she didn't move.

"The spirit is willing but the flesh is weak, right?"

"My flesh is still asleep. Would it be okay if I sleep-walked to the bakery?"

"Sure. I'll watch that you don't stumble into any canals."

Opening one eye, Sue looked up at me. "We really are in Venice, aren't we?"

I nodded.

She yawned. "Wow. I thought I'd had an elaborate dream. Don't go anywhere yet. I'm coming. Really. I'm getting up now." With determination, Sue rolled onto her back, lifted her tangled covers, and then fluffed them up in a billowy tent. She pulled the sheet and blanket up to her chin.

"What are you doing?"

"Making my bed." She completed the process by extracting the lower half of her body one leg at a time. "There." Smoothing the rippled covers, she stepped back to view her accomplishment with satisfaction.

"I'm guessing you're looking for another merit badge for that little achievement, aren't you?"

"That was kind of fun." She appeared to be more awake now. "I haven't tried that since Camp Fire Girl days, either. What about you? How did you sleep?"

"Great! Are you ready to find a bakery?"

"After you." Sue motioned to the stairs that led down to the apartment. We dressed quickly and quietly, hearing snores that reverberated from behind the closed bedroom doors. In our sleeping loft the brightness of the new day and the outside noises had awakened us. Inside the cooled palace, the closed shutters kept the interior dark and sheltered from the outside clattering. The men should sleep deeply for several more hours. Unless they were experiencing jet lag as well.

I wished I could take a warm shower and wash my hair, but we needed to get to the market, and I was afraid the noise of the running water would wake the others. Pulling on my wrinkled chinos and a clean shirt, I noticed how swollen my ankles were. I wasn't used to walking as much as I had yesterday. But I knew it was good for me, and I felt good.

Sue took a little longer to organize herself, but I could tell she was trying to hurry. Her hair was a monumental challenge. She managed to corral it into a ponytail, and we exited as quietly as we could.

We did fine making our way out of the building, but

once we were outside, we couldn't agree on the directions to the grocery store. My vote was to cross the bridge and turn right. Sue insisted we were supposed to cross the bridge and then go straight.

"Jenna, should I remind you about the hospital incident? Or will you just trust my sense of direction?"

Several weeks earlier Sue's mom had needed a ride to the hospital for some tests. I volunteered to take her and delivered her on time but to the wrong hospital.

"My car automatically goes to Southland General," I protested in the middle of the footbridge that led away from our palace. "After all the trips I made to Southland for Jack, all I have to do is put the key in the ignition, say the word 'hospital,' and my car goes to Southland on its own. It doesn't know how to get to St. Joseph's."

"All I'm saying is that you're better off trusting me with the directions."

"Hey," I said in playful defense. "You asked me to drive your mother to the hospital. I drove her to 'a hospital,' okay?"

"You're digging yourself a deeper hole, Jenna. Let's just say that we have different gifts, you and I. If it's directions we're wondering about during this trip, why don't we go with my instincts? Besides, I'm the one with the map now, remember?"

"I suppose you're going to try to earn a direction merit badge this morning," I teased.

We probably could have kept on with our sassy comments, but we had been walking this whole time and had to end our discussion because we were standing in front of the grocery store. Sue's instincts on the directions were right.

However, the store wasn't open. A panetteria was conveniently located across the way. Stepping inside, the delicious scent of freshly baked bread wafted our way and tickled our palates pink. Sue could chase down her favorite gelato all around town, but I'd be happy to sample every baked goodie at every one of Venezia's panetterias.

Two other people stood in line in front of us to order their daily bread. When it was our turn, I stepped up to the counter. Since I was the designated linguist of this expedition team, I started the conversation by smiling at the woman in the apron and saying, "Buon giorno."

"Buon giorno." She had golden hazel-colored eyes. I'd never seen eyes that color before.

I pointed at the round rolls that looked as if they were brushed with egg white on top to make them shiny. They were the most beautiful ones for sale. "Nine of these rolls, per favore." To make my order clear, I held up one hand with five outstretched fingers and on the other hand I utilized my thumb and first three fingers and said, "Nine."

"*Nove?*" She repeated.

"Si. Nove."

I pulled out some of the money Sam had sent me

ahead of time to purchase food. The change came back in coins along with the rolls wrapped up in a bundle of what looked like butcher paper.

"Grazie," I said, hearing the "r" roll slightly on my tongue for the first time.

"*Prego*," she replied, her expression warming.

Feeling confident and because no one was waiting behind us, I decided to further our conversation. In slow English I asked, "Do you sell coffee? Espresso?"

"*Caffe*?" Her answer after my nod was a long string of Italian.

"What did she say?" Sue asked.

"I have no idea. I think I know just enough Italian to be dangerous. She obviously thinks I understand her."

The woman seemed to be asking me a question. I gave her an apologetic shrug.

Sue stepped up and added a little dramatic interpretation. "We need to buy some *caf-fay* to take home." She acted out pouring coffee into a cup of coffee and drinking the hot beverage. Then she pointed out the door. "To go. *Caf-fay* to go. *Chow*."

She actually was quite entertaining, and I wasn't the only one who thought so.

The golden eyes of the amused woman crinkled in the corners. She held up her hand, as if indicating we should wait there while she went into the back. I hoped she had an English-speaking baker hiding out there.

Instead, she returned with a metal mixing bowl in her hands. I feared our communication triangle had failed. But then she showed us that the bowl was filled with fragrant ground coffee. With a smile she held out the bowl for us to take. I had the distinct feeling she had emptied her own coffee canister to provide for our need.

"Grazie, grazie," I said, holding out a ten-euro bill. I had no idea if that was enough.

"No, no," the woman said. She tapped the side of the metal mixing bowl and spoke the same phrase to us several times, looking at me implicitly.

I guessed she needed the bowl back so I said, "Si, si."

She nodded, appearing satisfied that we were of one mind on the matter. With a wave she said, "Ciao," and we were out the door.

"That was gracious of her," Sue said.

"I know. You don't find hospitality like that very often at home."

"It feels so different here," Sue said.

"Yes, it does." I was smiling the same way I'd smiled when we had arrived in Venice yesterday morning. I noticed that Sue wasn't biting her nails. That was a good sign.

Eight

Picking up the pace, Sue confidently led the way through the alleys and over the bridges. She successfully brought us back to our palace where the men were now all awake and gathered in the sitting room for morning devotions.

The late-night arriver to the group, Malachi, was standing by the wall tapestry, reading from the Psalms. His deep voice boomed through the air. "From the end of the earth I will cry to You…. For You have been a shelter for me, a strong tower from the enemy…. I will trust in the shelter of Your wings."

Sue and I slipped around the back way to the kitchen. We set to work, trying to figure out the percolator coffeepot. Eventually we placed it on the stove over a medium flame, and soon the rich Italian-roast fragrance filled the air.

Malachi's echoing words continued in rich, amber

tones. The cadence of his speech made it sound as if he were chanting the verses with a tribal sense of untamed authority. "The LORD looks down from heaven upon the children of men, to see if there are any who understand, who seek God. They have all turned aside…. As for me, I will call upon God, and the LORD shall save me. Evening and morning and at noon I will pray, and cry aloud, and He shall hear my voice…. O God, You are my God; early will I seek You; my soul thirsts for You; my flesh longs for You…. I will praise You, O Lord, among the peoples; I will sing to You among the nations. For Your mercy reaches unto the heavens, and Your truth unto the clouds. Be exalted, O God, above the heavens; let Your glory be above all the earth."

Sue and I both stopped our breakfast preparations and stood in reverence, not daring to make a sound while Malachi read. Never had I heard anyone read God's Word as if he believed every syllable. Without seeing Malachi's face, I still could sense that this man depended on the truth of every word as much as he depended on air, food, and water to sustain him.

Malachi ended with a crescendo of praise as he read, "Because Your lovingkindness is better than life, my lips shall praise You. Thus I will bless You while I live; I will lift up my hands in Your name. My soul shall be satisfied as with marrow and fatness, and my mouth shall praise You with joyful lips…. For You are my hope, O Lord GOD; You are my trust from my youth.... Whom have I in heaven but You? And there is none upon earth that I desire besides You. My flesh and my heart fail; but God is the strength of my heart and my portion forever. Forever and ever, amen and amen!"

"Amen," I responded in a soft voice.

The peace that surrounded us and filled up my senses at that moment was a peace so thick I felt that I could slice into it, chew it, and swallow it slowly.

Sue smiled at me. Her eyebrows were raised as she formed the word, "Wow."

I smiled back and nodded. "Yeah, wow," I whispered. "I didn't want him to stop."

"I know. But we need to get the rest of the food ready. Is there any jam or butter for the rolls?"

I opened the refrigerator. To my surprise, a dozen brown eggs in a bowl had appeared since last night.

Motioning for Sue to come see, I whispered, "Did you know about these?"

"No. Where did they come from?"

"I don't know. Do you think they were there before but we just didn't see them?"

"No, I would have remembered eggs. I'm very sure they weren't there."

I picked up one of them and shook it.

"What are you doing?" Sue whispered.

"It's hard-boiled. Let's serve these. Did you see those

fancy eggcups in the china cabinet? The painted glass ones? We could use those and serve the eggs with the rolls."

"Okay. Have you seen the salt and pepper?"

"Over there, on the shelf above the stove."

The fragrance of the percolating coffee filled the air, and the most wonderful sound filled the palace. The men were singing.

Sue paused to listen and then softly sang the old hymn along with them. I drew my shoulders back, hummed along, and placed the rolls for the continental feast on the dining room table. As I was filling the cups with coffee, the men entered and took their places.

Sue and I retreated to the kitchen and broke bread together. We ate in silence, each examining what the bread stood for in the full light that shone in our hearts.

The coffee was the best I ever had drunk. Sue said the same thing. She said the reason it tasted so good was because a stranger had given it as a gift.

"Hmmm," I said.

"Hmmm, what?"

"Showing love to a stranger. That's the definition of hospitality."

"It's humbling," Sue added a few minutes later.

"Humbling and beautiful," I said.

Sam entered the kitchen with an empty coffee cup in his hand. "Any chance we might have some more coffee? It's very good."

Sue and I smiled at each other and went to work, making more coffee and serving the men. On our side of this equation, it was a humbling and beautiful thing to show love to the strangers gathered around the table in the next room.

I carried the coffeepot into the dining room and filled the empty cups.

"Lovely breakfast," one of the men said as I poured the coffee for him. "Particularly the eggs."

"The eggs were a gift," I said. I noticed that Malachi lowered his eyes, as if trying to keep a secret.

When he came into the kitchen a short time later with several plates in each hand, I introduced myself and said, "Thank you for the eggs."

He looked surprised at my comment. I wondered if I had misjudged the situation. He lowered his eyes. "My wife was not favorable to my bringing the whole chicken."

I laughed. Malachi looked surprised again, as if what he had said wasn't meant to be humorous. I quickly sobered my expression and my spirit, realizing that Malachi probably had little to give. The eggs may have represented a great gift; he might have given the group the equivalent of a day's worth of food for his family in Kenya.

In an effort to cover at least some of my missteps, I said, "Please tell your wife we appreciate the sacrifice of the eggs."

Malachi looked at me as if I still hadn't grasped the situation. "The eggs were not a sacrifice. They were an offering. The chicken—now the chicken would have been a sacrifice."

His deep voice and unique use of English were fascinating.

"Well, then thank you for the offering," I whispered.

Malachi bowed to me honorably and left the kitchen.

In a sweet-to-the-spirit sort of way I felt as if I'd been in the presence of greatness.

Within an hour the men were in the midst of their strategy meeting, and Sue and I were back out the door on our way to the market. The morning was warming up, and the streets were filling with pedestrians.

Along the canal floated a sight that made Sue and me stop on the bridge and watch. A young man was paddling along in a raft. The two-person, blue-and-yellow raft held the man and two boxes of what looked like office supplies. He paddled up to a building across the canal from our palace and rapped his paddle on a small, low window about three feet above the water level.

The window opened, and another man reached out and received one of the two boxes. The deliveryman in the raft held up a clipboard for the man to sign a paper. The two exchanged friendly sounding words, and the delivery-man went on his way down the canal.

Neither of us commented on what we had just witnessed. The scene made complete sense. It was like the first time I saw a young man in a movie deliver a parcel in downtown San Francisco by riding his bicycle into an office building.

With a growing sense of comfort in our surroundings, Sue and I walked back to the panetteria first and returned the silver bowl with smiles and many mixed "grazies." Sue was the one who suggested we buy several loaves of the fresh-from-the-oven *ciabatta* bread to accompany the main meal. It smelled so good I wanted to tear into it before we left the bakery. Again the bread was wrapped in brown butcher paper, and we carried it across the way to the grocery store.

As soon as we entered the *mercato,* I felt strangely at home. The grocery store I worked in was two or maybe three times the size of this store, but the layout was similar. Checkout stands by the front door, produce on the right side. Using handheld baskets instead of wheeled carts, shoppers easily navigated the narrow aisles. Sue and I effortlessly figured out the basics like eggs, butter, milk, cheese, chicken, and of course, coffee.

But Sue had a short list with several items that I argued we didn't need. She insisted she had plans for them and picked up fresh garlic cloves, a bunch of fresh basil, a small block of Parmesan cheese, whipping cream in a small bottle, and more olive oil.

While standing in the checkout line, we realized we

were facing a small challenge. We hadn't brought our own shopping bags like the locals had. Apparently when one shops in Venice, one brings her own bags. Now I understood why the store didn't provide large, wheeled carts for shoppers to fill. Everything that was purchased had to be carried home.

Improvising, Sue and I loaded our shoulder bags with the items. What we couldn't fit in our purses, we loaded in our arms.

A young woman, observing our balancing act, pointed to a peg at the front of the store from which hung netted bags. They looked like colorful macramé beach bags. We soon found that the netting weave allowed the bag to expand and to hold various-shaped items. We gladly bought four of the bags and filled them with our groceries. It was the only time during our stay in Venice that we arrived at a market without those indispensable bags.

"Are you willing to have a little adventure?" Sue asked as we exited the store.

"That depends. Does it involve carrying these groceries very far?"

"Not much farther. I want to try another route home. I think the next street over takes us straight home, but we'll see a different street."

"Okay," I said. "You're the navigator. Go ahead. Impress me with your sense of direction."

Sue led the way. We passed a shoe store and a TV

repair shop and then came to a shaded corner where a bar occupied one side of the street. Directly across from the bar was an open-air fruit stand displaying a beautiful array of summer fruits under a dark blue canopy.

We walked up and admired the variety and freshness of the fruit.

"Look," Sue said. "Apricots. Your favorite. Let's get some. We could fit a few into these grocery bags, don't you think?"

"Sure. They look so good. And look at these tomatoes."

The older man behind the stand seemed to sense my admiration for the fruits and vegetables. He picked up one of the regally purple eggplants and polished it with a cloth, glancing up at me in a flirtatious way to see if I noticed the extra care he gave to his produce.

"Jenna, I think we should load up with all we can manage to fit in our bags, don't you? We have room."

"Four zucchini, please," I said, easily catching the man's attention by holding up my thumb and three fingers. It seemed like a good idea to start with the item that had the same name in English as it did in Italian.

"*Quattro* zucchini," he repeated briskly, ready to assist me.

"Si."

Sue pointed to the nectarines. "Could you ask him for five of these?"

I gave her a funny look. "You can ask him as easily as I can."

"He'll understand you better." She gave me a pitiful look that seemed to say, "Please don't make me drawl in public again."

Turning to the merchant of Venice, I held up five fingers and pointed to the nectarines with a big smile. He said something in Italian and placed the nectarines on the scale.

"See, Sue? I didn't say a word, and he understood. You could have done that."

"Uh, I think maybe you should have used some words. He's up to nectarine eight and counting."

"No." I briskly moved my hand back and forth and held up five fingers. "Only five. No more. Only five."

"Si, *cinque chilli.*"

"*Kee-lay?*" Sue repeated.

"Are you saying 'kilos'?" I asked. "No, not kilos. Just five nectarines. How do you say 'only'?"

"Don't ask me," Sue said.

"*Solo?*" I questioned the merchant, taking a stab at the word for 'only.' "Solo five nectarines. Solo cinque…"

"Solo?" he repeated, appearing amused.

In what I'm guessing was her idea of on-the-spot assistance, Sue sang, "*O solo mio!*"

The produce merchant burst into laughter. "*Gondolier!*" he called out to the other man in the booth, pointing at Sue.

"No, she's not trying to imitate a gondola driver," I said. "We want only five nectarines, okay?"

Now both of them were talking to us and about us, I'm sure. They were grinning and elbowing each other as they watched us wilting under the intense Italian dialogue. The older one tilted his head back and imitated Sue, singing, "*O solo mio*." He actually was pretty good.

The younger man leaned over as the concert continued and said something to me that included the phrase, "cinque chilli."

"Fine," I said, giving up. "Si. Cinque chilli."

He looked proud of himself, as if he had solved the language problem between all men and women and every warring nation since the beginning of time. Nothing is as mesmerizing as the face of a proud Venetian. Sue and I watched as he jubilantly weighed out five blessed kilos of ripe nectarines while his pal sang.

I didn't dare try to add apricots to our order.

Nine

Heading back to our palace at a brisk pace, Sue and I could still hear the fruit vendors loudly singing another chorus of "*O Solo Mio*."

Sue chuckled and glanced at me. I didn't think the situation was that funny, and apparently Sue could tell that by my look because she pressed her lips together, as if to hold in a laughter bubble.

We ducked around the corner and could *still* hear the duet. A giggle leaked from Sue's lips.

I smiled ever so slightly, remembering the proud look on the vendor's face as he weighed the fat nectarines and sang at the top of his lungs. That certainly never had happened in the produce section of Abbot's Grocery! I tried to picture our skinny produce guy singing to the customers, and a chuckle rose in my throat. The chuckle escaped my mock serious expression, and the minute it did, Sue's rumbling belly laugh exploded.

"They're still singing!" she said between laughs.

I had to stop walking. All I could do was laugh. Sue and I put down our heavy bags and tried to catch our breath between the shoulder-shaking laughter.

Neither of us could speak for several minutes. The tears rolled down our cheeks, and the giddy-fest kept going. I couldn't recall the last time I had laughed so hard and consequently felt so good.

When we caught our breath, we lugged the bursting bags of groceries to our palace. Trickles of giggles trailed us like invisible streamers.

Both of us said later that the nectarine encounter wasn't *that* funny, and the merchants of Venice actually were kind of rude to mock us. But once a contagious laugh bug latches onto you, if you aren't up on your chuckle inoculations, you could well end up with the giggles—and you'll get them bad!

We were out of breath by the time we carried the groceries up the marble stairs. I thought my arms were going to fall off. Later we found out that five kilos of nectarines were equivalent to eleven pounds. That plus all the other groceries.

"No wonder all the Venetian women we've seen are so slim," Sue said. "If I had to do this every day, I'd be svelte, too!"

Her use of the word *svelte* made me feel another bout of laughter coming on. I turned away from her and tried to think of something serious so I wouldn't give way to the giggles again and disrupt the men. Their voices echoed in the other room as their strategy meeting continued.

Sue and I composed ourselves. We dropped the grocery bags onto the counter, and then we dropped into the two chairs by the open window. I still was smiling as a slight breeze floated in and tended to the beads of perspiration coursing down our necks.

"Do you want some water?" Sue forced herself out of the chair.

"Sure. Thanks."

She filled two glasses and then turned around with one of the freshly plucked fruits in her hand. "Nectarine?"

"I hate nectarines," I said with a straight face.

"You do not."

"Yes, I do. Of all the fruits we could have bulked up on, nectarines are my least favorite."

"You're serious, aren't you?"

I nodded.

Sue looked like she still was riding on the giggle endorphins as she swished across the floor. "Ah, but you've never had an Italian nectarine that has been blessed by a singing merchant of Venice!"

"No, and it's possible I never will."

"Aw, come on. You should at least try one." Sue rinsed

a nectarine and took a big bite. "Mmm. So delicious. Fresh and sweet and—hey! I wonder if they make gelato out of these. We'll have to ask next time. Where's your phrase book?"

I pointed to my lumpy shoulder bag that rested on the marble-top table where I had hoisted it. Even my purse had become a receptacle for the nectarines.

Sue thumbed through the small book. "Here it is." She pointed to the words *pesca nettarina* and pronounced it aloud, "Pes-ka net-a-ree-na."

She paused, thinking a moment. "Hey, wasn't that the name of a Soviet figure skater?"

I couldn't help it. I burst out laughing again. Covering my mouth, I tried to lower my voice so the men wouldn't hear. The way Sue pronounced the words did make them sound like a Soviet figure skater.

Sue looked pleased that she had cajoled another laugh from me. "The next time we go for gelato I'm going to ask for pes-ka net-a-ree-na and see what I get."

"You do that," I said, rising and calming myself. I concentrated on placing the perishable groceries into the refrigerator because I knew it wouldn't take much for Sue to start me laughing again. In an effort to move the conversation onto a more serious topic, I asked, "Did I tell you that I found out where the eggs came from?"

"No, where?"

"Malachi brought them."

"All the way from Africa?"

I nodded and told Sue what Malachi had said about the chicken being the sacrifice and the eggs being only an offering.

"Makes you think, doesn't it? We have so much," Sue said.

"I know."

"I think I complain too much, Jenna."

"Why do you say that?"

"I'm not very thankful for the little things. The gifts, or I guess I should call them offerings, that come my way every day. Not to mention all the sacrifices. My way of thinking about everything the past few years has been through the Jack-filter, if you know what I mean. I think of Jack's situation every hour of every day, and everything else in my life is measured by the aftermath of his accident. It's too easy to feel sorry for myself."

I stopped rearranging the items in the refrigerator and gave Sue my full attention. She seemed to sense my intense interest in what she had said and quickly pulled back. "I'm just thinking aloud."

"I know. That's okay."

"You don't have to diagnose me or anything."

"Diagnose you?"

"You know, like you did the other day, when you figured out why I didn't want to sleep on the couch."

"Oh."

"Or when you wanted me to pray with you on the roof, and I said I'm still figuring things out."

"That's okay." I looked away, trying to give Sue the space she was asking for. I knew then that I had invited her on this trip because I wanted to "help" her. I wanted her to get away from her situation at home, and yes, if I were completely honest, I thought I could "fix" her. There. I admitted it to myself.

What I sensed in the kitchen that morning was the Spirit of God refreshing my sister-in-law through everything around us. We had been washed with the Word as Malachi read from Psalms, then all the new experiences, tastes, encounters, and small challenges were displays of how God could care for Sue more than I ever could. My job wasn't to diagnose her or counsel her or try to teach her anything. We were students together. Equals in every way. Sue and I were fellow victims of grace.

I felt as if I'd just been shown my place—a clarification of my role in our friendship in this new season of diving into the deep end and experiencing the refreshing that comes from such a plunge. I had places deep inside me that I needed to examine and that needed healing, too, but Sue wasn't trying to fix those in me. All I had to do was be here and receive the grace as it fell on me.

I smiled at Sue.

She smiled back. A relieved expression lessened the worry wrinkles that had shown up on her forehead. She could take the next breath, the next step in her spiritual journey with a sense of freedom.

I felt free as well.

"So, what should we do first?" Sue looked around the kitchen. "I guess I could cut up some of the nectarines and put them out on the table while the meeting still is going on."

"Sounds like a good idea."

We took our positions, and the dance of the kitchen maids commenced. Sue washed the nectarines, sliced them, and placed them on the table in three small plates before I had found enough places to store the rest of the groceries.

We went to work preparing the midday meal. Organized Sue had brought a cookbook of Italian recipes with her. It's a good thing I didn't know that before this moment because I would have made fun of her.

However, she had a plan, and I didn't. Having measurements and directions in front of us in English was a lifesaver. I, of course, hadn't even considered what we would cook or how we would know what amounts to prepare.

Sue suggested we round everything up to servings for ten, wanting to make sure there was enough. She also had thought through the menu options and had purchased all the ingredients necessary for chicken scallopini.

"Doesn't *scallopini* refer to veal?" I asked. Not being much of a cook, I was out of my element.

"It just means the meat is thin. And you pound it."

"What do you mean, 'you pound it'?"

Sue looked at me in disbelief. "You know, you cover the boneless meat with wax paper or plastic wrap, and then you pound it with a mallet until it's thin and tenderized."

"Really?"

"You've never done that? You've never made pork chops or chicken like that?"

"No, never. I told you I'm not a cook." With a half a tease I added, "Now do you understand why I asked you to come with me?"

Sue reached for the aprons we had left on a wall hook the night before and with a stiff arm held out one of them to me. Then she slipped on her apron with a new determination and gave the strings a tug as she tied them.

"Watch and learn, Jenna, girl. We are going to make some art out of this dead chicken. And brace yourself because I'm thinking of incorporating a few nectarines in the experiment."

Newly empowered in the kitchen, Sue went to work, making use of the tools available to us. In lieu of wax paper she employed the butcher paper that our bread had been bundled up in. When she couldn't find a mallet or meat tenderizer, she told me to stand back. Removing one of her shoes, she rinsed the sole with hot water and used the flat heel to pulverize the boneless chicken thighs between the butcher paper.

"Do we cook all this in the oven?" I asked.

Sue looked at me as if I were making a joke. "Jenna, we don't have an oven."

I looked around and for the first time realized the kitchen wasn't outfitted with an oven. How could I have missed that detail? How were we going to prepare food for all these men without an oven?

"That's why we're making scallopini," Sue said. "We have three frying pans, and we're going to need all of them. Could you pull those out?"

She continued giving me directions, which I noticed was a role she was enjoying. "We're serving lunch at noon, right? Because once we start to cook this, we need to serve it right away."

"Yes, they said noon. Should I set the table so it's ready?"

"Great idea. And bring the plates into the kitchen. We'll serve the scallopini directly on the plates. You can wash the zucchini after the table is set. Cut them into really narrow pieces. We're going to steam them."

"Okay." I was a willing assistant to my organized sister-in-law.

The final result of her creativity was masterpiece quality in my eyes. At noon she and I stepped into the dining room carrying plates that artfully displayed our offering to the men.

The thin chicken thighs had been floured, braised,

covered with a cream sauce, and accented with thin slices of the fresh nectarines. The companion, steamed zucchini, filled out the china plates with color and texture. Appreciative murmurs rose as we delivered the hot plates, and the men began to eat.

As if all that clever deliciousness wasn't enough, Sue had made fresh pesto from the bunch of basil, garlic, and olive oil. I'd never seen anyone use a mortar and pestle before. She handled the beautiful marble set like a medieval herbalist. Two small bowls of the pesto were placed at either end of the table next to the two loaves of bread.

I stood back and watched the men eat, making sure we had placed everything on the table that they needed. Slipping back into the kitchen, I smiled at Sue. She grinned back and nodded. Mission accomplished.

We had just finished putting away the last pan when Sue pointed to the round clock on the wall. "It's only one-thirty. What do you want to do now? Please say you want to go shopping."

"Do we need more groceries already?"

"No, we have everything we need for the meal tonight," Sue said. "I meant window shopping. Fun shopping. Or we could just walk around and see some of the sights."

"Shopping is at the top of the charts for me," I said, equally interested in taking advantage of the open space in our schedule. Before Sue mentioned shopping I'd been thinking a little siesta sounded inviting. However, our beds were going to be in the sun all afternoon. Our only place for a siesta would be in the two chairs here in the kitchen by the window.

I was beginning to realize that I was an early morning bird who liked to take off flying and then return to her nest to tuck her head under her wing halfway through the day. Sue was the afternoon bunny who took awhile to wind up, but once she got going, she was energized.

"I thought I'd pull out the map and chart an easy course for us," Sue suggested.

"While you do that, I'm going to sneak into the shower."

"Okay. Do you care where we go?"

"No. I'm interested in seeing anything and everything."

Instead of reviving me, the shower exasperated me. The trickle of water from the handheld nozzle was more of a sprinkle than a shower. I washed and rinsed my short hair as best I could. The next time I washed my hair I'd use the kitchen sink.

"That was fast," Sue said, when I returned to the kitchen in clean clothes and fluffing my wet hair with a hand towel.

I gave her an evaluation of the shower situation, and she gave me a list of exploring options. The possibilities were neatly listed and numbered in her new notebook. On the map she had numbered different regions of Venice to correspond with the list.

"You're amazing," I said. I never would have thought to do something that organized. "Which option do you recommend?"

"I was thinking the Rialto Bridge area over here. See? It's not too far away, and there are lots of shops."

"Sounds perfect. I would love to find a skirt."

"Me, too. And some cooler blouses."

She looked at me and took a little sniff. "You smell so good now, Jenna. Fresh from the shower. I may need a little refresher before we head out. I'll be fast."

"Take your time." I pulled one of the chairs over to the open kitchen window and estimated it would take less than five minutes for my hair to dry in that spot. I loved sitting alone in the quiet, catching occasional phrases from the men in the other room. Malachi's voice was the most distinct.

I closed my eyes and leaned into the sunlight. In a private moment of bliss, I allowed my mind the luxury of tumbling around a few thoughts. Was my life characterized by "offerings" or "sacrifices"? Did I even try to give anything to others?

Of course I did. I moved to Dallas to give my brother and Sue time and help and encouragement. That had been a sacrifice, hadn't it? I'd left my daughter and my home and a familiar life. Yes, familiar but small.

In some ways, had I merely traded one small, secure life for another equally small, safe life?

I wasn't disturbed by the questions. It felt good to ask them. The only nudging in my spirit was the old 3 a.m. thought about not being "done" yet. For some reason this trip to Venice didn't seem as if it was going to be "it," whatever "it" was.

Floating into a relaxed and sleepy state, I was content to know that I wasn't "done" and that this trip wasn't "it."

Ten

S ue entered the kitchen as I was dropping into that cushy layer of sleep where it felt like my muscles were floating in a warm bath.

"Ready?" she asked softly, touching my shoulder. "Or do you want to sleep some more?"

I blinked. "No, I'm ready. I'm awake." I was so relaxed I could have fallen into a deep nap the way I had the day before and slept away the afternoon.

"The air seems heavier during the afternoons here." I drew in a deep breath and stretched my neck. "If you stop moving, it feels as if the air covers you like an invisible blanket."

"You do look relaxed," Sue said.

Forcing myself to rise from the chair, I watched Sue tie up her wet hair with a bandana. A wide smile lit her face.

"What?" I checked the side of my mouth to see if part of my "relaxed" look included drooling while I had slept.

"Nothing. I'm just happy."

"You are?"

She nodded. "This is great, Jenna. All of it. Walking to the grocery store, the singing guys at the fruit stand, cooking these creative meals…not to mention washing my hair in a marble sink."

Her smile was matched by a glistening of tears. That's when I knew Sue was "here." All the way.

"Thank you, Jenna, for inviting me to come with you. I know I've said that before, but I really mean it. You had a lot of friends you could have asked to come and help you to cook for these guys. Thanks for asking me."

"You were my first choice, Sue." As a tease I added, "Of course, it does help that you actually know how to cook."

"Even so, you didn't have to ask me."

"Well, I did. And I'm glad I did. So, are we ready to go shopping?"

"Born ready."

Once we were on our way, I was more awake. Sue directed us confidently down the main route to Paolo's and the Strada Nuova. I noticed she avoided the side street with the corner fruit market. The first shop we came to was closed.

"Steph wasn't kidding," Sue said. "It looks as if all these shops do close in the afternoon. I'm hoping that if we head toward the more touristy areas, we'll find shops that are open."

A few more minutes of walking along the main thoroughfares brought us to a string of English-speaking, Visa-accepting shops. Their doors were wide open. Dozens of carts covered with colorful souvenirs were positioned strategically in front of the shops. Masks of all shapes and colors hung from the carts.

Sue and I stopped at the first cart, and Sue picked out a bright red mask that had a long, bird-like beak. She held it up so that her eyes appeared in the oval eye slits.

"That's kind of creepy."

"What about this one?" She exchanged the bird mask for a frowning face that looked like the "tragedy" mask often seen with the "comedy" mask as a universal logo for theater.

"Depressing," Sue said, mimicking my frown. "What are these made from? They're so hard."

"Papier-mâché," the vendor said as he sat on a stool watching the foot traffic go by. He answered us over his shoulder without looking directly at us. We had become accustomed to people around us not understanding English.

"Oh, thanks." Sue returned the mask to the hanging hook.

We wandered to the next cart and bought a few tiny trinkets—key chains in the shape of little gondolas, a few bookmarks, and some postcards. Several hawkers who were displaying leather purses and an odd assortment of pottery called to us as we walked past their blankets of goods spread out on the street.

To avoid their pleas, Sue and I stepped into a clothing store. The salesclerk seemed to size us up and determine our nationality instantly. She greeted us, "Good afternoon. Everything on the two front racks is on sale."

Sue and I went through all the sale items. Nothing caught our eye, so we said "thanks" instead of "grazie" and moved on to the next store.

A green cashmere sweater prompted Sue to pause and gaze in the window. "That is gorgeous, but I need cooler clothes. Where are the summer cottons?"

The salesperson standing just inside the doorway with a cell phone held to her ear obviously understood Sue and pointed us to the rack of summer items inside the store. We went through the rack and reached for skirts at the same moment. Holding them out for examination, we realized we each had selected the same style skirt but in different colors.

Sue laughed. "Are we going to have to call dibs on these?"

"Why? They're different colors. Let's try them on." Hers was a light cocoa-brown color. The one I held up was a deep blue.

We shared a mirror in the dressing room area that was separated from the store by a fabric curtain. The skirts fit both of us perfectly.

"Bella," the saleswoman said when she stepped into the changing area to check on us. Translating, she repeated, "Beautiful on you. Would you like to see some blouses to match?"

Before we could say yes or no, she left the dressing room and quickly returned with several blouses for us to try on. I decided not to even put on any of them since I had brought enough cool blouses with me.

"So, what do you think of this one?" Sue asked once she buttoned up the second selection.

"I liked the first one better. This one is too wide across the shoulders. It looks funny. Try on the third one."

Sue ended up buying two of the blouses: a blue one and a cocoa-brown shade that nicely matched the skirt. I purchased just the skirt.

I understood why Sue was so eager to buy the tops, though. Not only did she need cooler options to wear, but also with her skin tone and hair, she was more limited in the colors that looked good on her. Both the blouses looked fabulous on her.

"If y'all don't mind," Sue said to the salesclerk, "I'd love to wear this out of here. To go. Do y'all let people do that? Wear clothes out of the store?"

"Of course." The salesclerk removed the tags from Sue's skirt and the cocoa blouse and then turned to me with her small pair of scissors.

"Go ahead, Jenna. Wear your skirt, too."

"Okay." I never had worn clothes out of a store before, but why not?

Making our way to the Rialto Bridge a few moments later, Sue and I displayed a new swish to our walk.

"I think we should celebrate our shopping success with a new flavor of gelato, don't you?" Sue asked.

"I was wondering when you would suggest that."

The crowds of pedestrians thickened as we approached the Rialto Bridge. Caught up in the crush of people, Sue and I moved with the crowd over the wide expanse while dozens of languages swirled around us. Hundreds of people passed each other on the covered bridge, and we were jostled about like bumper cars at a fair.

On both sides of us, rows of stalls were set up to sell kitschy trinkets and fresh vegetables to the obliging visitors. And although I couldn't see fish stands, the odor in the heat of the afternoon made me think the fish market had to be nearby as well.

Sue and I didn't pause at any of the stalls but stayed close, keeping our purses even closer. This place felt like a million miles away from our palace neighborhood and the quiet Campo Apostoli.

A few minutes later, as we stood in line at a gelato

stand, we looked back on the covered bridge and began to appreciate its size and beauty. Symmetrical, arched windows ran the stone expanse's length. The bridge itself was arched and as impressive as any Renaissance cathedral. Gondolas and various other boats floated beneath it.

"So many people," Sue said. "I didn't expect so many people here."

"Do you want to pass on buying gelato here and find another place?"

"No, this is okay."

As we waited in line, the afternoon heat seemed to rise up from the walkway in invisible flames.

"This is the most expensive gelato so far," Sue said, as we contemplated the list of flavors.

I noticed the line behind us was now a dozen people long. "They sure do a good business here."

"Do they have nectarine?" Sue asked. "I forgot how to say it."

I scanned the list for pesca nettarina but didn't see it. We each ordered a single scoop and then stepped out of the flow of tourist traffic to find a place to eat. It wasn't an easy task. The Grand Canal was only a few feet away, but no place had been provided to sit. We were pressed on every side by sweaty, irritable tourists speaking half a dozen languages.

"This is crazy." Sue pulled back from the crowd and led me down a less congested alleyway. We stood under the awning of a shop that sold spices. The display in the window was a collection of small bowls on varied tiers, with each bowl containing a different spice or herb in its natural state with a hand-printed sign beneath in Italian. The only one I recognized was oregano. I imagined this shop looked exactly the same for the last half a millennium.

"There has to be another route back to where we just came from. Here, hold this." Sue handed me her cup of gelato and pulled out the map.

I dipped my plastic spoon into her melon gelato and gave my rating on the spot. "Oh, this is nice. I'd give this one a 9."

"I'm giving it a 3." Sue didn't look up from the map.

"A 3? Why?"

"It tastes like cantaloupe. I don't like cantaloupe."

"Are you just saying that because I said I didn't like nectarines?"

"No, I don't like cantaloupe."

"So why did you pick the melon flavor?"

"To get it over with."

I made a face at my wacky sister-in-law. "You don't have to order the ones you don't like, you know. You have lots of other flavors to choose from."

Sue ignored me and turned her full attention to the map.

I helped myself to another spoonful of melon gelato and gave an appreciative "mmm."

Looking up at me sideways, Sue said, "I can see you're enjoying this research as much as I am."

"I'd say I'm enjoying it more," I said with a playful smirk. "But that might have something to do with my ordering flavors I think I'll like."

"Go ahead; tease me all you want. I made the decision under pressure."

"What pressure?"

Sue squared her shoulders. "I wanted to order for myself. The word for *melon* looked like I could pronounce it, so I ordered it because I figured I wouldn't completely mess up how to say it."

"Oh, Sue." I was about to tell her that of all the gelato stands we would visit that one definitely had employees who would have understood English as well as French and German and probably Japanese since it was located in such a high-traffic tourist area. Instead I said, "Do you want to trade?"

She looked at my gelato. "What did you get?"

"Fior di latte."

Her eyebrows rose.

I translated roughly based on my impressions from my first taste. "Vanilla."

"Okay, I'll trade. But next time I'll have you order for me, and I'm going to pick the most exotic flavor on the list."

"That would probably be the *pannettone con zabajone*."

"And what is that?"

"I have no idea. I saw it on the list, but I wasn't brave enough to try it."

Sue tilted up her chin. "Well, that's what I'm selecting next time, and if you're nice to me, I just might let you have a taste."

"Well, fine. And if you're nice to me, I just might let you pay for it."

With our noses in the air, we strutted back across the Rialto Bridge.

Eleven

The rest of our second full day in Venice followed a rhythm close to that of the previous evening. We returned to the apartment and prepared pasta for the men. They gathered in the elegant dining room, and we served them wearing our not-exactly-matching, matching skirts.

Cleanup was a little more complicated because the water went off around nine o'clock for some reason. The timing couldn't have been worse. We had just begun to wash the dishes. We found other things to do in the kitchen and kept checking the faucets. By ten o'clock we gave up and left the pots and plates until morning.

Climbing the stairs to our rooftop hideaway, I felt as if my feet were going to fall off, they were so sore. I'm sure they were swollen. In that one day I think I walked more than I had walked during any given week back home. At work I'm on my feet all day, but standing is quite different from walking.

Pushing open the door to the roof, Sue and I climbed out into the calm coolness of the night. Everything was as we had left it. Even the grinning moon and the field of sprouting stars.

"Oh, dear little bed, I don't think I've ever been so happy to see a mattress and covers," I said.

"Ditto for me," Sue echoed.

We crawled under the covers. I don't even remember saying good night.

The sun came on tiptoes and crept over the edge of our loft the next morning. I felt the steady, warm fingers touch my face as if they were gently patting me awake.

Squinting to see my watch, I read the dial. Six-thirty. Same time as our sunny wake-up call the day before. This morning the streets didn't seem to be as alive with sounds as the day before. Either that or the sound of wooden hand-pushed carts rolling over cobblestones was becoming more familiar.

I rolled over and was surprised to see Sue already awake. She was propped up on her elbow and cradling something in her hands.

"Hey, good morning, early bird," I said.

"Shh. Look. Here's the real early bird." Sue turned slowly, and I saw a small mass of dark gray and brown feathers sticking out of her cupped hands.

"How did you catch a bird?"

"I didn't catch her. She fell on me. I was sound asleep, and then I felt her small thud on my rear end."

"Soft landing." I laughed.

Sue looked at me with a wary smile. "I was thinking the same thing. My padded backside might have saved this little bird's life."

"It's still alive then?"

"Yes." Her voice was soft. "I can feel her little heart beating."

"Are sure it's a girl?"

"No, but I'm calling her a girl." Sue held the tiny intruder out for me to see the slight twitching of its beak. "Do you think I should let her go?"

"I don't know. Why don't you put it down and see what happens?"

Sue placed the fallen sparrow on an open space at the end of her mattress and pulled back her hands. "There you go. Can you fly?"

Sue's feathered friend gave what looked like a shiver, attempted a hop, and sat down on Sue's blanket.

"Poor thing! Let's find a box and make a nest. We can keep her in the kitchen until she's better."

"Are you trying for another merit badge?" I asked.

"What?"

"You know, our midlife merit badges we were joking about. I wondered if you were going for a bird-saving merit badge."

Sue wasn't in a joking mood.

As we padded around looking for a suitable container, we tried to be quiet in the kitchen. The waxed cardboard box that the green beans had come in was still in the trash. I pulled it out and lined the box with bits of paper towel.

"Didn't Steph say the trash had to go out to the sidewalk before eight on Tuesday?" Sue asked.

"That's right. I'm glad you remembered. I'll dress and take down the garbage."

Sue eased the bird into the box. Again it gave a little shiver and then hunkered down, looking exhausted.

"I hope it's going to be okay," I said.

"Me, too."

I stepped over to the sink and tried to turn on the water. "Oh, good. We have water this morning." I filled the sink to wash the stacked-up plates and pasta pots.

"I can do those," Sue said. "You better take out the trash and go to the bakery before the men wake up."

"Are you sure you don't want to go to the bakery with me?"

"I'll stay here and start the coffee."

I dressed quickly, feeling sore after all the walking yesterday. The soreness was good, as if my muscles were saying, "Hey, thanks for remembering what we're here for.

We can do a whole lot more than you give us a chance to."
With a few stretches, I was ready to go.

As I placed the trash bags on the sidewalk, a neighborhood cat prowled through the pile of bags. I shooed it
away. But as I tromped over the bridge, I wondered if a cat
could have traumatized the little bird.

I liked being up early and being more familiar with our
neighborhood. When I entered the bakery, the golden-eyed
woman greeted me with a warm, "Buon giorno!" I wished I
understood Italian and could converse with her.

"Buon giorno," I replied and then tried an awkward,
"*Grazie per le caffe*…yesterday. Thanks again for the coffee
you gave us yesterday."

She said something and pointed to the back room. I
thought she might be offering more coffee, so I quickly
said, "No. No caffe. Grazie. Solo…"

I pointed at the breakfast pastries in the case and
smiled, hoping she would get the idea I only wanted to
buy some rolls.

She pointed to a tray of fresh-looking rolls that were
different from the ones she had offered us from the top
shelf the day before. Today's special looked like rectangular
croissants with a dab of chocolate peeking out the sides.
The hand-printed sign next to them displaying the cost
had the word *baci*.

"Solo baci today. No coffee." I pointed to the rolls.

"Solo *uno* baci?" She held up her thumb.

"No. Uh…" I tried to remember the word for *nine*. I didn't want to get caught in the opposite tangle of the five kilos of nectarines and return with only one roll to share between all of us.

"I need nine." I held up my fingers, remembering to include my thumbs. Someone entered the store behind me, but I didn't turn to look. I didn't want to lose my concentration.

"Nove? Nove baci?" she asked.

"Si. Nove baci. Per favore."

She quickly blew nine kisses at me with the palm of her hand.

I didn't move.

She was smiling broadly, as if pleased with herself and some sort of joke that I obviously didn't get.

"I'm sorry," I said, my best nervous grin taking over my face. "I don't understand. *Non capisco*." I thought that was how to say I didn't understand, but now I was wondering if I should avoid using any Italian unless I was confident I knew what I was saying.

The customer behind me spoke up. "The bread you order. It has the same word for 'kiss.' Baci. She is making for you nine kisses. Do you see?"

"Oh." I turned and found myself face-to-face with a gondolier. His straw hat was under his arm, but the striped shirt he wore gave away his occupation.

"She knows you want the breads. She is only making

for you a joke. We call these breads 'kisses.' You see?"

"Yes, I see." I turned and offered her a smile of under-standing. Looking back at the gondolier I said, "May I ask you a favor? Could you please tell her thank you for the coffee yesterday?"

He stepped closer and rattled off my message as the woman rolled four baci at a time in the butcher paper. She responded kindly without looking up at him.

"Lucia says you're welcome for the coffee."

"Lucia," I repeated, nodding at her. She smiled back.

The gondolier added, "You must be hungry this morn-ing. That is many baci—many 'kisses' for one woman."

Not sure if he was trying to flirt with me or make fun of me, I defended my kisses by saying, "They're not all for me. I'm serving seven men."

Well, that was the wrong thing to say! Especially to a gondolier who made his living from cruisin' and schmoozin' with the tourists. He made a motion of shaking out his hand, as if I were too hot to handle. Then he trans-lated my comment to Lucia.

Like a loyal friend, Lucia took her cue from my reac-tion to the gondolier's "hot mama" innuendos and didn't act amused. She looked at me as I paid for the bread and asked something in Italian, pointing at me.

Again I was at a loss.

"Your name. *Nome.* She wants to know your name," the gondolier translated.

"Jenna."

"Yanna," she repeated.

It was close enough. Apparently *J* is not a commonly used letter in Italian words. I nodded, took the change from her, and received the bundles of fresh "kisses." "Ciao, Lucia. Grazie."

She responded with something that sounded like "dough-money."

I was obligated to turn once again to our suave wordsmith.

"*Domani*. Tomorrow. Tomorrow you will be here? She wants to know."

"Si," I said, smiling at Lucia. "Domani. I will be back domani with some more dough money." Now I was the one making a goofy little joke she wouldn't understand.

"Never mind." Lowering my head, I eased past our interpreter with a polite nod. He wasn't ready to let me slip out.

"So, Yanna, when you and your seven men need a gondolier, you come to me. I will show you Venezia." He explained where I could find the district for his gondolier stand, but I didn't recognize the location.

"Grazie," I said.

"Prego."

I gave Lucia a final grin over my shoulder and was on my way.

Trotting quickly with the warm rolls in my arms, a

slow smile danced across my lips. Sue would be sorry she missed this day's visit to the bakery.

I carefully inserted the key into the ancient lock of our street-level door. As I turned the key, the door opened. I love it when doors open the first time.

Stepping over the threshold with my arms full of kisses, I paused. As crazy as I knew it was, I held the door open a little longer, waiting so that goodness and mercy had plenty of time to catch up and follow me into the damp darkness.

Making my grand entrance into the kitchen with our daily bread, I told Sue my morning panetteria story, complete with lots of hand motions in true Italian form. She and I split one of the warm baci while I talked.

Sue asked, "What did you say after he told you to come looking for him?"

"He wasn't saying for just me to come. He said to bring everyone for a gondola ride."

"Right. So what did you say to him?"

"I said grazie."

"And what did he say?"

"He said prego. Then I left."

Sue looked stumped. "Prego? Like spaghetti sauce. That's what he said to you?"

I curtailed my chuckle. "*Prego* is Italian for 'you're welcome.'"

"Oh." Sue unwrapped the rest of the breakfast rolls. "I

was hoping he had said you could count on a big discount. You and all seven men."

We chuckled quietly. In the dining room we could hear the men shuffling in and assembling for breakfast.

"The coffee is on the table for them," Sue said, quickly placing the last roll on the platter. "I'll take these out."

"Did I miss devotions?"

Sue nodded.

"Did Malachi read more psalms like yesterday?"

She nodded again, this time smiling.

"Bummer," I muttered. "I'm sorry I missed it."

Sue slid into the dining room with the platter heaped with fresh kisses from the bakery. I'm sure these men never had dined on such sweet manna gathered on such a gorgeous morning.

Since I was alone, I playfully imitated Lucia's cute joke and blew "baci" toward the dining room with the palm of my hand. One, two, three, four, five, six, seven for the men gathered together to break bread. And one extra big baci for Sue.

I had just flung my palm toward the dining room when I realized I wasn't alone.

Twelve

One of the men, Sergei, was standing in the kitchen behind me. I was sure he had seen my last blown kiss. I'd delivered the playful smacker to the closed door with as much gusto as if I were a contestant on the old *Dating Game* TV show.

Apparently Sergei had entered by the kitchen's back door that led down the hall to the bedrooms and the princess suite. Before I could say anything to him, Sue entered through the dining room door.

"I have this for the bird," Sergei said to Sue. He held out some cotton balls that looked like the sort that are stuffed into the tops of vitamin bottles.

"Perfect. Thank you."

I rolled into the topic at hand without considering for a moment the option of explaining to Sergei or anyone else why I was blowing kisses.

"How is the bird?" I asked quickly.

"The same, I think." Sue walked over to the box balanced on the wide window ledge. She set to work, tucking the cotton around the edges of the new nest. "I can't see that she's injured anywhere. But she keeps shivering."

"Did you put some water in there for her?" I peeked inside the box and saw the answer to my question. "Is that the top of a toothpaste tube? Very clever."

"I'm glad you think so because it came from your toothpaste."

"Mine?"

"My toothpaste has a flip top. I hope you don't mind."

"Not too much. What did you do with the toothpaste tube?"

"I put it in a seal-top bag. I had an extra one."

I brushed off the confiscation of my toothpaste lid and only halfway paid attention to Sue's answer. I was more interested in watching Sergei slip out of the kitchen and join the others in the dining room without giving me a second look.

"This will be the true test to see if our bird is female." Sue sprinkled crumbs from her chocolate-filled baci into the bird's box. "If she goes for the chocolate, we'll know her gender."

The bird gave a little shiver and ignored the crumbs altogether.

"Maybe she's in shock," I suggested.

"I wonder what happened to her," Sue said.

I told Sue about the cat I had seen earlier when taking out the trash.

"Don't you worry your feathers about a thing," Sue crooned to the small creature. "You're safe here with us. We'll take care of you, little Pesca Netareena."

"What are you calling the bird?"

"Pesca Netareena. I asked Sergei, and he said it wasn't the name of any Soviet figure skater he had ever heard of."

I remembered then the jokes we had made the day before about Sue's pronunciation of the Italian word for nectarines. "Sue, you crack me up."

She seemed pleased with herself.

We fell back into our roles as scullery maids and started the preparations for the rest of the day's meals. Again our rhythm came to us easily. We cleaned up after the continental breakfast and hurried out to the grocery store. This time we had sufficient bags with us to carry all the necessary ingredients to make spaghetti with meat sauce for lunch and a big pot of minestrone soup for the late evening meal. We were getting our routine down.

We joked on the way back from the grocery store about whether we should stop by the fruit stand corner. Sue said she was sure that, if the same vendors were at the stand, they would break into song at the sight of us. We decided not to find out.

Little Netareena seemed to have sipped some of the

water while we were gone. Either that or it was evaporating as the warmth of the day rose. Aware that today was much warmer than the last two days, we went to work cooking what we could while it was still morning.

I prepared the meat sauce while Sue readied the rest of the meal. We served right at noon and had everything cleared and cleaned by two o'clock. Sue wore her energized look and said she was ready to change into her swishy skirt and hit the cobblestones.

I told her I was ready for a nap.

"Are you too tired to go out? We don't have to go anywhere today," she said, looking wistful.

"Yes, we do. We're in Venice. Of course we have to go somewhere this afternoon. I want to see whatever we can. I just don't know where you get your afternoon energy."

"I don't know where you get your top o' the morning energy, so we're even."

It didn't take long for us to change into our "sightseeing" skirts and slip out of the apartment with all the makings for the minestrone soup waiting for our return. Sue had placed Netareena's box nest on the kitchen's floor in a shady corner. That way the little bird could stay cool during the afternoon siesta, and if she did try to hop out of her nest, it wouldn't be such a long drop.

"Do you have a plan for us, or are we going to just explore at random?" I asked.

"A little of both, I think. I was looking at the tour book

while you were at the bakery, and I wondered if you would mind visiting some of the churches and art museums."

I wasn't much of a museum buff or an art lover. I preferred admiring the solitary trees of Venice or gazing at the varying shades of blue in the water. That was the sort of art I appreciated. Perhaps I'd been to too many European art museums when I was young. Now I was complacent about them.

However, all this was new to Sue, and I didn't mind looking at paintings with her. Or visiting some of the Venetian churches. Sue seemed to have a deeper appreciation for the arts. She understood what made certain strains of music beautiful or what made marble so valuable. I was sure I could learn much from her.

"I thought we would start with the *Accademia*. The tour book said it's one of the main museums. It's farther away than the Rialto Bridge, but I think I've figured out a shortcut on the map."

For a moment I considered backing out because I wasn't excited about walking for miles on the hard, uneven walkways. But if we didn't go now, when would we? And if I didn't go, Sue probably wouldn't. This was our chance; we needed to take it.

We exited our building and stepped into the bright sunlight. Sue stopped to make sure she had her sunglasses.

On the walkway in front of our apartment, a woman passed us pushing a tiny baby in a stroller. I made eye contact with her and smiled at her little bundle of wonder. The mother gave me a shy half nod.

With resolve I said to my willing-and-able tour guide, "Okay, you lead the way. I'm ready for whatever."

I didn't know it then, but my words would turn out to be an unexpectedly important step of faith for me. Just as I was being asked to follow Sue on our afternoon adventure, so too would I be asked to follow the Lord into the unknown adventure of the next season of my life. But at the time I barely had a hint of what was to come.

With Sue, I could easily see each step coming. She referred to the map often as we wound through the maze of alleyways. Once we were in motion, I was caught up in the sights, sounds, and scents all around us. My sore feet and tired legs were ignored.

Sue was pretty proud of herself when we arrived at the front of the Accademia via her shortcut. She liked maps and puzzles; this was her kind of adventure. Once we were inside the huge art museum, she seemed to see a map to follow or a puzzle to solve in every painting. We had lots of discussions about different pieces, but none of the paintings drew me into its mystery the way each one lured Sue.

Many of the compositions were obvious. Portraits of once famous Venetians, Madonnas of all sizes, and depictions of the crucifixion were the recurring themes. All the art was beautiful. I enjoyed looking at it but had no trouble turning and walking away. Sue, however, stood close to the pictures and came out of the Accademia with the marvels of the Renaissance reflected on her face. She looked positively enlightened.

The bonus of the afternoon was a church we came upon after we walked over the tall, wooden Accademia Bridge. I never did look up in the tour book which small church it was. We would have marched right past it, as we had so many of the other churches in Venice, but this one had opened its doors, revealing cool, uncluttered pews waiting inside. Weary, warm afternoon visitors were welcome to enter and listen to a string ensemble playing a soothing concert of baroque music. Apparently the musicians were practicing for that night's concert.

Sue entered first, drawn like a moth to its mother flame. She and the musical notes flitted close to each other. I entered like the kind of moth that goes right to the electric bug light and gets zapped. As soon as my weary bones settled into the pew, I closed my eyes and slept contentedly in the lulling presence of the same music that caused Sue to sit up straight and lean forward.

"Refreshed?" Sue asked me when the practice ended and I opened my eyes.

"Yes. Definitely. You?"

She nodded. "That was amazing. Absolutely amazing. Did you hear the second violin on that last stanza?"

In all honesty, I hadn't even realized there was more than one violin. But I *was* in the church while the music was being played, and I did have my ears unplugged, so I somewhat truthfully answered, "Yes, I heard it." Then, to redeem my generalization, I added, "But I'm sure I can't begin to appreciate any of this music the way you can."

"I just appreciate your coming with me."

"Sure."

Sue checked her watch. "We better get back to start the soup. Oh, what an incredible afternoon!"

I was glad Sue liked the art and the music. That side of her had never been pampered like this at home.

We had gone the equivalent of about three blocks when Sue said, "Hey, look!" She picked up her pace and made a beeline to a gelato stand. A listing of flavors hung from the top of the window.

I knew what was coming next. "Okay, which one do you want me to try to pronounce?" I asked.

"You're off the hook," she said, scanning the list. "They have tiramisu here. I don't remember seeing that flavor before. I'm going to try tiramisu, and I even know how to pronounce it."

"I love tiramisu. I'm going to try that one, too."

We both gave the tiramisu a perfect 10. The first and only perfect score issued during our week of careful examination.

As Sue and I approached the Ca'Zen, with our bellies sated from the tiramisu gelato, we saw Sam and Bruce. They were coming from the opposite direction.

We waved and met up with them by the canal that ran in front of our place.

"Looks like we have an adjustment to our plans for the evening," Sam said. "We just connected with a friend of Bruce's, and we've been invited to take a picnic out on an evening boat ride."

"Oh," Sue said. I guessed she was calculating quickly how to change the planned evening's meal into sufficient picnic food for the men to take with them.

"The boat ride isn't only for us," Bruce said. "You two are invited to come as well, if you would like."

I'm sure my expression lit up. "Yes. Thanks for including us."

"We'll have to hurry to the grocery store to buy some food," Sue said.

"Buy more food? You won't have time," Sam said. "We're planning to meet Marcos at the dock in fifteen minutes."

Sue looked panicked. "But we don't have picnic food ready. We were planning on soup for tonight, and we can't take that with us, so we'll have to go to the store."

"No." Sam held up his hand before Sue went any further. "I'm sorry I didn't make myself clear. Our host is providing the picnic. All we have to do is show up."

Sue started to breathe normally again. I smiled as yet another gift of hospitality was presented unexpectedly to us.

With a quick chance to run up to the apartment and

grab a sweater, we were back out the door. Sue, me, and seven bodyguards. Who needed a gondola when we had a private boat coming for us?

Our grand procession tromped to the *Fondamenta Nuove*, which was the same area where Sue and I had eaten at the waterfront restaurant our first afternoon here. We arrived a little early and waited at a small dock. Dozens of boats bobbed and scuttled their way across the lagoon. One of them, a long, open-seated boat with an elevated prow, pulled into the dock. The young man steering the boat into the narrow parking spot greeted Bruce with loud shouts. Bruce grinned back at his enthusiastic friend.

As soon as Bruce was on board, the young man embraced him soundly, and the two of them shared a rousing reunion. Bruce introduced all of us to Marcos. Greeting us by looking us each in the eye, Marcos shook hands all around.

The seating was tight for the nine of us. Sue and I were barely in our spots when Marcos backed up the boat and motored out onto the chopped-up water. It felt like we were anchovies being thrown into a mixed salad. All of the men leaned back, smiling and taking in the salt spray on their faces, as if they had waited a long time for this experience. Sue and I sat close in our new skirts, feeling the goose bumps race up and down our bare legs.

Sue's hair began to dance. She tried to pull it back, tie it up, tame it in any way she could, but it turned into a fiery octopus sitting on her head, taking over. She gave up trying to control the friendly monster and laughed as the sea spray misted her face.

Bruce stood next to Marcos at the helm. The two shouted their conversation. It was in English, and I picked up enough to understand that Marcos's father owned a jewelry store in Venice. They were talking about a mutual friend, Todd, who lived in California. I'd done plenty of pondering lately on how large the world was outside my small life, yet here was a smallness. A small circle formed by a man from South Africa who knew a young man from Venice because they both knew someone from California. That sort of close-knit circle was only possible to create inside the borders of a large life.

Sam's earlier comment, when he explained that the picnic had been provided for us this evening, came back to me. He had said, "All we have to do is show up."

I hoped I could remember that thought later because I wanted to write it down and think some more about it. All I had to do was show up.

When I was twenty, I led a large life. I was in Venice now because of a friendship formed when my life was wide open to endless possibilities. After so many years of small-ness, now I wanted to see the borders of my life expand once again, as they had so many years ago.

We cruised past a small boat with two young boys who weren't happy about the wake Marcos's boat caused. I watched them over my shoulder, and they made sure I saw their lewd gesture.

The boat continued around the perimeter of the main island. To our left, land stretched for as far as I could see.

"Lido," Marcos shouted to Sue and me, pointing to the island. "It's very long and narrow. This island protects the lagoon from being swallowed by the sea. Venezia, she is married to the sea, you know. They have lived in harmony for fifteen hundred years. That is a good marriage."

I smiled to myself at Marcos's comment. Apparently I wasn't the only one who thought of Venezia as a woman.

She was stunning that evening. The sun's golden light across the waters reflected Venezia's best attributes and dimmed her flaws.

"Are you saying people have lived here since the fifth century?" Sue shouted into the wind so Marcos could hear.

"Si. When Attila the Hun invaded Northern Italy, people from the mainland came to these islands. This is a good place for defense. For more than twelve hundred years the Venetians lived here undefeated as an independent republic."

"Then what happened?" Sue asked.

"Napoleon. Venezia surrendered to Napoleon in the late 1700s. She had no choice. Fifty years after that Venezia gave herself to Italy for protection, and here we are. Still she remains the devoted partner of the sea. And still we are her devoted children, floating in this lagoon on petrified logs."

"I read something about the petrified logs that hold up parts of the island," Sue said. "Isn't there a church built on a million logs cut on the mainland and sunk into the lagoon?"

Marcos didn't hear Sue's question because he was busy at the moment, maneuvering our low-riding vessel into an expanse of water that was thick with other boats. We must have been heading west because the setting sun was now in front of us.

To the left, across the water, another island lay close at hand. The domed church and tall tower that dominated the island were constructed with the same red-tile roofs and the same wheat-colored walls as many of the buildings in the neighborhood we were staying in. But these structures, set against the primrose sky, seemed to soak in the evening sun, warming by degrees as the sun slipped lower. It was the kind of scene often shown in movies or painted in oils. It made me feel as if I had seen it before.

On the right side of the boat, San Marco Square came into view, resplendent in the golden light. I held my breath. She was so beautiful.

The pale stone of the Doge's Palace along the waterfront took on the rosy glow of a young woman's complexion. The symmetrical, arched windows of the long palace appeared to gaze at their reflection in the dimming waters. At the entrance to San Marco Square, a row of ebony gondolas lined up between tall poles, looking like eager piggies nudging their way closer at dinnertime.

This was the image of Venice that graced tour books and calendars. *Piazza San Marco*. This was the face of Venezia, and she was magnificent. Still proud. Still unspeakably beautiful after all these years.

Thirteen

"*Look at that! Just look at that!*" Sue said, expressing the admiration I was feeling as we gazed upon Piazza San Marco at sunset. "I have to start taking pictures." She reached into her shoulder bag for her camera while I stared, trying to sear the image on my memory.

I doubted any camera in the world could capture the way the evening light shrouded Venezia's face in beguiling mystery.

"That must be the bell tower." Sue pointed her camera at a terra-cotta-colored structure that rose from the open square on our right. The narrow building was topped with what looked like a triangular-shaped hat that gave it the appearance of being ready to make a rocket shot to the moon.

"I read about the bell tower in the tour book," Sue said.

"It collapsed a hundred years ago, but they rebuilt it."

From the boat we could just catch a side view of the entrance to San Marco Basilica. The great rounded domes of the eight-hundred-year-old church caught the evening light like a cluster of low, rising moons.

Sam leaned over and pointed out the partial view of the basilica to Sue and me. "San Marco is the best example of Byzantine architecture you'll see this side of Istanbul. Are you planning to take a tour?"

"Definitely!" Sue answered for both of us.

"What church is that?" I pointed to a huge, white-domed church rising from a peninsula to the left at the opening of the Grand Canal.

Sam didn't know, so he called on Marcos to fill us in. We were motoring slowly in this high-traffic area, which made it easier to hear Marcos and easier for Sue to snap dozens of pictures.

"*La Basilica di Santa Maria della Salute*," Marcos said, the words rolling off his tongue. "This one is only four hundred years old. It was built in thanks to God after the plague came on Venezia. Not so many of the Venetians died as in other parts of Europe. To offer thanks to God for so many survivors, they built this church."

"Is it the church that's built on a million petrified logs?" Sue asked.

Marcos looked at Sue with admiration. "Si. Very good. Yes, a million. Maybe a million and one. They say the builder drank too much *vino,* and he lost count. Could be a million and two."

I was the first to smile at Marcos in acknowledgement of his joke. He turned to me with a chin-up sort of grin and gave me an appreciative wink. I smiled, thinking how adept every Venetian man was at flirting, regardless of the woman's age who received the benefit of his charms.

Without warning, a pervasive sadness came over me. The sharp sting of this melancholy was familiar, but I hadn't felt its forceful pull in a long time. Yet it didn't matter that I had put those emotions far away from me. The feelings were elemental. The longings were easily recognizable.

I wanted to be loved. I wanted to be married. I wanted to be married to a man who loved me and wouldn't leave me.

There, I admitted it. In such a place as this on such a night as this, I wish I didn't have to be alone. I wish I weren't so alone. I wish my life hadn't gone the way it did.

The tears came before I could stop them.

Turning my head as far away from the others as I could, I pretended to carefully examine the water and the distant island. I actually was deep inside myself, standing on the edge of an emotional precipice. These feelings nearly had overpowered me more than once in the past. I knew what it meant to look down into such darkness.

An evening breeze skimmed across the lagoon and dried my tears as quickly as I shed them. For a few moments I let myself wish that a wonderful man would fall from the sky into my life. I wished he would find me irresistible, sweep me up in his arms, and love me forever.

I blinked back the self-pity tears and tried to remember what I had taken away from those counseling sessions so long ago. The counselor had given me a potent weapon to use in moments like this: thankfulness, a grateful spirit.

I tried to think of one thing for which I was thankful. I knew that, with a handful of darts forged from a spirit of appreciation, I could take down dragons of doubt and vultures of self-pity.

It took a moment before I was composed enough to pick up the first dart and throw it at the target of my deep longing.

"This," I whispered. "All of this. I'm thankful for this—the travel, the experiences, the people."

"Jenna, you okay?" Sue touched my arm.

I nodded and gave her a smile I almost meant.

She didn't look convinced. What she did next was tender. However, I appreciate it more now than I did at the time. She moved closer to me on the seat. That's all. She just snuggled closer. We already were sitting close, but she moved closer, like a pillar, sitting up straight and offering her steadiness, if I wanted to lean on her for a while.

Then she went on interacting with the others as if no one else needed to know that I was having a "moment," as she called it when we talked about it later that night.

But there on the boat, she sat close, and I leaned into her just enough until the emotional flash of loneliness dissipated.

The boat entered the Grand Canal at a dawdling pace. None of the men seemed to have noticed my brief tears. Marcos turned over the steering of the boat to Bruce.

Motioning for several of the men to stand, Marcos lifted one of the seats and pulled out our picnic. We all assisted in passing around the bountiful supply of provolone cheese, thin-sliced ham, tiny sweet tomatoes, and huge green olives in a canning jar.

As we ate, Marcos, with lots of hand motions, launched into a personalized tour of all we floated past. He told us how Venezia had been a main center of trade between the East and the West. His favorite hero was Marco Polo, the invincible explorer who left Venezia at the age of seventeen.

"He was gone for twenty years. When he returned, he brought to his Venezia silks and spices from China. This made her the wealthiest city in Europe for hundreds of years."

As Marcos went on, I found it difficult to discern what was fact and what was Marcos's fiction. He seemed to enjoy putting his own spin on every story associated with the famous and infamous Venetians.

We heard about the notorious spy and statesman, Casanova; the brilliant composer, Vivaldi; and Tintoretto, the painter whom Marcos considered the most under-appreciated artist of the Renaissance. Marcos even had a recommendation for where we could see the best collection of Tintoretto's paintings.

"The Frari Church," he said with an authoritative air. "*Magnifico!*"

"I need to write that down." Sue pulled out her notebook. "We saw one of his painting at the Accademia. The painting showed some men stealing a man's body. Do you remember that painting, Jenna?"

I did remember the painting. It seemed as if the grave robbers were about to run right off the picture.

Marcos once again was impressed with Sue's familiarity with his beloved Venezia's history. "Si, Tintoretto. Do you know whose body they were stealing?"

We shook our heads.

"I will give a hint. Whose bones are enshrined at *Basilica di San Marco*?

"The Apostle Mark," Sam said.

"Si. Of course. San Marco. This is a famous story, in the Tintoretto painting, and it is true. Some Venetians, they sailed to Alexandria and stole San Marco from his grave. The men smuggled his remains out of Egypt in a barrel. Across the top of the barrel they put the word *pork*. You know why they do this?"

Without waiting for us to speculate, Marcos supplied the answer. "The Muslims in Alexandria would not touch pork. It is unclean to them. They would not touch the barrel. And then the men, they wrap the holy relic in the sail of their ship and return to Venezia. They present this great gift to the Doge, who is the ruler of all Venezia, and he built the church, the Basilica di San Marco to honor the relic."

"Really?" Sue seemed to be trying to determine if Marcos was exaggerating. "You're saying the actual bones of Mark, one of Jesus' disciples, are buried inside that big church?"

"Si. Of course. This is why you see so many of the lions in Venezia. The lion with wings is the symbol for San Marco. For Saint Mark. This is all true, what I am telling you."

Sue glanced at Sam, and Sam nodded at Sue. "According to tradition, yes, Mark's remains are buried here."

"You can also see a Tintoretto at *San Giorgio Maggiore.*" Marcos seemed to have no end to his knowledge—or at least his stories—about sites in Venice. "The Benedictine monks are there. They have been at this church for centuries."

Fikret leaned forward and asked if the Benedictine monks still were active at San Giorgio Maggiore.

"Si. Some say the good lives of the monks are what has kept the…how do you say *cattiveria?* The bad, very bad, from destroying Venezia. Capisce?

"Yes," Sam answered. "We know what you mean. The prayers of a few have often been known to spare the many from destruction."

Fikret asked if the Benedictine monks held regular prayer times at the church and if the services were open to the public.

Marcos shrugged and looked chagrined that he was stumped by a question. He replied with a line of thought familiar to him. "San Benedicto was Italiano, you know."

Fikret turned to the other men. "This is what I brought up at lunch today. The four rules of the Benedictine order: prayer, community, work, rest. Are these not the fundamentals by which each of us still structure our lives of ministry?"

An agreeable discussion followed as Marcos maneuvered the boat into the same docking area at Ca'd'Oro where Sue and I had disembarked from our first vaporetto ride Sunday morning. Only this time we had traveled up the Grand Canal from the opposite direction of the train station.

The dark, silky shroud of night was being pulled around the city. I felt as if now we had encircled the roundness of Mama Venezia and had seen a few more of her many moods. She was amazing. Unmovable. Resilient and determined, despite her age.

"This is the final story for you," Marcos said after he eased his father's boat into the narrow dock. "You see this building with all the decoration? This is the finest Gothic building in Venezia, the Ca'd'Oro. Gold is *oro*, si? This is the Gold House because the outside was once covered with so much gold. The gold is gone now. Who knows? Maybe the gold has washed with the rain back into the canal. Maybe it has gone into the air. Maybe all of us Venetians breathe this gold and drink of it a little every day for many years, and this is how we come to have our good looks."

We all grinned, and a few of the men applauded Marcos for his final story. I found myself involuntarily drawing in a deep breath, as if some of those gilded flecks might find their way into me.

Our merry band said our good-byes with strong hugs and respectable kisses on the cheek for Sue and me. We headed down the dark alleyway and came out on the better-lit Strada Nuova. I had the feeling again that goodness and mercy were following us. I turned around once, quickly, as if I could catch them before they hid from view, but they were fast. Really fast. I just wanted to tell them I liked having them around, and I wanted them to stay close all the days of my life.

Approaching Paolo's outdoor café, Sue said, "If any of y'all are interested in stopping for a coffee, Jenna and I can recommend this café here on the corner."

One suggestion was all it took. Coffee wasn't something this group had to be convinced to stop for.

Soon we had three tables pulled together and were

gathered in a huddle, ready for more food and more conversation, two of the great attributes of the Venetian lifestyle.

The men still were talking about St. Benedict. Fikret told us how this Italian monk lived in a cave outside of Rome. He eventually directed twelve monasteries and wrote a book outlining instructions for the men who lived at those monasteries. What amazed me was that all this happened more than fifteen hundred years ago. Yet the same principles of prayer, community, work, and rest were the four pillars holding up this week for all of us. More than ever I felt honored to be part of this time with Sam and his band of brothers.

The waiter approached our assembly and addressed us in English. He was quite a bit younger than Paolo, who appeared to be missing this evening. I supposed Paolo needed to go home sometime. Perhaps this young man was Paolo's son.

All of us ordered coffee except Sue. She hesitated and then finally agreed to coffee as well.

Our coffees came, but I noticed that Sue couldn't stop fidgeting. The moment I saw her nibble on what was left of her thumbnail, I leaned over. "Go ahead. Order some gelato. You know you want to."

Sue gave me a look of mock surprise. "How did you know that's what I was thinking?"

I rolled my eyes.

She cleared her throat and jumped into a brief pause in the conversation. "I have another question for y'all. I'm working on an independent research project and…"

We ordered gelato all around. In an effort to be helpful, of course.

Each of us selected a different flavor and agreed to report our evaluations to Sue. It was hilarious listening to these studious men try to seriously, or maybe not so seriously, appraise the gelato.

"I found the pistachio to be crunchy like a nut," Peter said. "Write that down."

"The limoncello is like a lemon," said Eduardo. "Only with sugar."

Sue put down her pen after Sergei from Ukraine described his amaretto as "cold."

All the men laughed good-naturedly and serious Sergei finally gave way to a half grin that I was sure he had been hiding ever since he had caught me blowing kisses that morning.

I decided then that some secret delights will never be understood by the male species. Such joys are best shared only between girlfriends and should never be revealed to the unappreciative.

I leaned over and whispered to Sue, "I think it's a Sisterchick thing."

She nodded her agreement and dropped her notebook back into her bag.

Fourteen

The next morning Sue made sure little Pesca Netareena had enough crumbs and water before joining me in our daybreak jaunt to the panetteria. I was eager to see what delicious treats, fresh from the oven, Lucia had this new day.

Sue was eager to see if the gondolier would be there again. She was disappointed. I was not.

The bakery special of the day came in square, flat loaves. Lucia told us the name three times. "*Schiacciata alla Amaretto.*"

When none of the words rang any bells for me, she cut a slice for us to try. The rich, dense, egg-batter bread sandwiched a thin layer of almond paste, and sliced almonds topped it all.

"Delicious!" I nodded at Lucia to let her know we would take all four of the loaves she had on the counter.

She seemed pleased and talked earnestly to us in Italian. I hate to admit it, but at that point, I missed the gondolier. We needed an interpreter. My guess was that she was telling us why this was a special recipe. It seemed she had gone to extra effort to prepare the bread. I expressed, in English, my appreciation.

"We should buy a couple of bread loaves for lunch," Sue suggested. "To go with the minestrone soup."

Pulling out our money, I pointed to several loaves. We purchased more bread than we needed, but it all looked and smelled so good. Plus I felt as if each loaf had been baked with sweet care. How could we possibly walk away from Lucia's offering?

Lucia grinned broadly and asked me a question that included the word *domani*.

"Si," I answered. "Domani. Ciao!"

"Did you actually understand her?" Sue asked as we waved good-bye.

"I think she asked if we'll be back tomorrow, and I said yes."

Sue and I took off, looking like robbers who just had held up a bread store and didn't have enough hands to carry the loot.

When we entered our palace apartment, all was strangely quiet.

"I have a feeling we missed Malachi's reading," Sue whispered.

I made a pouting face. My disappointment at not hearing Malachi read from the Bible again was greater than I expressed outwardly. I listened for any sound of the men and wondered if they were in the sitting room at the front of the apartment having a time of quiet prayer.

Sue and I tiptoed through the back hallway to the kitchen. Netareena chirped from her nest, providing the only sound in the apartment.

I put down the shopping bags and looked through the open door into the dining room. No one appeared. Walking through the dining room, I checked the large sitting room.

"No one is here," I told Sue when I returned to the kitchen. "Or else they're still sleeping."

"I doubt that. It's late."

"This place is awfully quiet when no one is around."

Just then we heard the sound of slow, muffled footsteps on the marble floor. The sound came from down the hallway that led to the princess suite. Sue and I exchanged wary glances.

"This is like that Nancy Drew book where Nancy and Bess were in the mansion and..." I didn't finish my whispered thought because the footsteps were louder now and definitely coming toward the kitchen.

Sue and I stared at the door, waiting for it to open.

The footsteps stopped, and Sue reached for one of the kitchen knives on the counter.

I mouthed the word "Sue!" and gave her a scowl.

She put her finger to her lips, her eyes wide, fixed on the closed door.

I could feel my heart rising to my throat where it thumped soundly.

The kitchen door opened slowly. Sue put her arm across the front of me, as if she were about to protect me from whatever would pounce on us. In her other hand, she raised the knife.

"Sue!" I whispered.

The door opened all the way, and Sergei timidly peered into the kitchen.

Sue dropped her arm and the knife. She flipped her hair behind her ear as if nothing unusual were going on. "Morning!" she said a little too brightly.

"Good morning." Sergei looked at me and then at Sue. I was sure our wild-eyed first expressions must have told him something was wacky. Again. Of course, if he noticed the raised knife in Sue's hand as he entered, then he definitely figured out we were nuts.

"It's so quiet," I said, more as a weak explanation of our strange behavior than as a conversation-starter.

"The others have gone," Sergei said.

"Gone where?"

"To morning prayers at San Giorgio Maggiore. Were you still with us last night when the group decided to go this morning?"

"No, we went straight to bed," I replied. "We must have missed hearing about the plans."

"I'm sorry we didn't know." Sue pulled herself into a more normal posture and expression. "We could have prepared something for them to eat before they left. Was it a problem that breakfast wasn't ready for them?"

"No, they took breakfast with them."

"They did?"

"The fruit." Sergei pointed to the empty bowl that had been spilling over with nectarines the night before. "They hoped it would be all right."

"Oh, it's more than all right." A relaxed grin returned to my face.

"Good. I stayed behind to make a call, and I left my phone in here to charge." He reached for the mobile phone that was plugged into an outlet above the sideboard.

"We have breakfast bread now," I said as Sergei turned to leave. "It will be here in the kitchen if you want some."

"Thank you. I will come back."

"And I'll make some coffee," Sue called out.

Sergei left, and Sue turned and playfully fwapped me across the midriff.

"Hey! Why are you hitting me?"

"Because you had me going with all your Nancy Drew, 'Mystery of the Vacant Venetian Palace' stuff."

"Me!? You were the one with the butcher knife!"

"It's not a butcher knife. Look at it. That's just a dull bread knife."

"What were you planning to do? Butter him up?"

Sue ignored my pun and sputtered, "Well, I was all creeped out. I thought we were going to have to run for our lives!"

I laughed. "And just where would we have gone?"

Sue eased up and shrugged. "I don't know. The bakery. Or maybe the fruit stand. Those men would have protected us."

"Right! Once they started singing at us, our assailant would have fled for sure."

We had a good laugh. I decided I liked the kitchen much more when laughter echoed off the high ceilings. The silence was a little creepy in such a large place.

As if invited to now make noise, Netareena chirped.

"That's a good sign." Sue went over to the nest. "I think she's laughing, too."

"How's she look?" I asked.

"She's not moving much, but at least she's chirping."

Sue made coffee, and the place felt even more awake and homey instead of somber and mysterious. I sliced the almond bread into generous wedges since we had so much.

We took our breakfast goodies into the empty dining room. The two of us sat across from each other at the large table, ready to eat, but it seemed as if something was missing.

"I feel like we should read from the Bible for our own morning worship," I said. "It won't sound anything like Malachi but..."

"It's a good idea," Sue said. "Did you see the Bible over there on the chair?"

I picked it up and looked inside. It was Malachi's Bible. The cover was worn. Some of the pages were torn or stained. I opened to the Psalms and slowly turned the pages. Every page of the book had handwritten notes in the narrow margins. I felt as if I were looking into someone's diary.

"I feel like I'm being intrusive," I told Sue, holding the Bible so she could see what I meant. A thin slip of paper fell out and floated to the table.

"A Bible that's falling apart usually belongs to a person whose life isn't," Sue commented. "My mother used to say that. Her Bible looked like that, too."

I picked up the note that had fallen out. It appeared to be a handwritten schedule with the dates of the retreat across the top. Under each date was a list of verses. "If this is Malachi's note, then today he was going to read John 21. He wrote, 'Breakfast by the Sea' and 'Jesus Restores Peter.'"

"Go ahead," Sue said. "Read the chapter. You don't have to read any of his personal notes in the margins. Just read the verses."

I turned to John 21, the final chapter of that gospel and read about impulsive Peter and how he jumped out of his fishing boat to swim to shore because Jesus was there, waiting for him beside a small fire.

When I got to verse 12, I read, "Jesus said to them, 'Come and eat breakfast.'"

I looked up, and Sue was smiling, too, at Malachi's choice of verses.

"They were having fish and bread for breakfast," Sue noted. "I'm glad we skipped the fish and just went with the bread."

I carefully returned Malachi's Bible to the chair where I had found it and tucked the note back inside. Then I gave thanks in a smile-laced prayer. Sue and I broke almond bread together and talked about what we should do that day.

"What about going to Murano?" She glanced up at the intricate chandelier over our heads. "I'd love to see how they make something like this."

I had studied the chandelier a number of times since first entering the dining room. Each time I saw a different color or pattern in the vibrant, blown-glass masterpiece.

"We could go this morning," Sue said. "We could start the minestrone soup, then we could leave for a couple of hours and come back to heat it up when it's time to eat."

"Okay. What do you need me to do?"

Before Sue could answer my question, Sergei entered the dining room and nodded a greeting to both of us.

"Are y'all ready for some coffee now? I'll get it." Sue hopped up.

Sergei took a seat and glanced at me timidly. "I think my wife would like it here."

"I'm sure she would like it here very much."

Returning from the kitchen Sue added, "I think any woman would love Venice."

"Venice, yes," Sergei said. "But I have seen how happy the two of you have been these few days, and I was thinking how much my wife would like to laugh with you."

"This trip has been like medicine for both of us, hasn't it, Jenna?"

I nodded, glad to hear Sue felt that way.

Sergei's expression remained serious. "My wife works very hard for long hours. I think she needs more friends. More friends that are not heavy to her heart. Do you know what I am saying?"

I nodded, feeling a tug at my heart for Sergei's wife. I knew all too well the feelings of isolation and the need for a female friend who understood. My circumstances over the past few decades may have been different from Sergei's wife, but the feelings of loneliness were, I'm sure, the same.

"Where do you and your wife live?" Sue asked.

"Kiev. In Ukraine."

"What mission organization are you with?" I asked.

Sergei said the name in Russian, and I stopped breathing for a moment. My reaction must have been obvious because Sergei said, "Have you heard of us? We are not very large. I do not think we are known in the States."

Finding my voice I said, "No. I mean, yes. I know your mission. I…"

"Jenna, are you all right?" Sue asked. "You're turning pale."

I drew in a steady breath and looked at Sergei with my heart pounding. "I know your mission very well." My voice was quavering. "I worked at the German office a long time ago."

"When?" Sergei leaned forward.

"It was a long time ago. Thirty years. I went…I took… It was back when the borders were still closed and—"

"You were a courier?" Sergei finished my sentence for me. His voice was low, as if KGB might be in the other room listening.

I nodded.

His eyes widened.

"Y'all just lost me there," Sue said. "What's a courier?"

Both of us hesitated. My training at the mission as a twenty-one-year-old was explicit about protecting the believers in the underground churches. The fewer people we told the fewer chances of putting the persecuted Christians at risk. In the past thirty years I had told only a handful of people about how I had agreed to go with another woman into countries that, at the time, were ruled by Soviet Russia. We made the journey with nothing more than God's protective hand on us and a memorized address of a believer who was willing to receive our delivery.

"What do you mean by courier?" Sue repeated.

"A courier is a smuggler," I said.

Sue looked at Sergei and then back at me. "What did y'all smuggle?" She didn't look as if she really wanted to know. But I told her.

"Bibles."

"You, Jenna? You smuggled Bibles?"

I nodded.

"What year was it?" Sergei asked.

"I'm trying to remember. It's been so long."

"Did you come by train?"

"No, I drove a camper with another woman my age. A young German woman."

Sergei leaned across the table, looking stunned and then strangely delighted. "You came with Deborah."

"Yes! Did you hear about us?"

"Of course. You were the two young women who did what many men could not do."

Feeling as if I could at long last spill the story from my closed-up, alabaster box, I turned to Sue and explained, "Some of the men who worked for the mission were caught at the border when they tried to take in a few Bibles. The mission had more than five thousand Bibles ready to be delivered, but no couriers who could make it through with so many Bibles."

Sergei added, "Only a few willing couriers worked on the German side. They had their passports stamped too many times with the same countries of entry. The guards always were suspicious."

Sue's mouth was frozen in a dropped open position. She barely was blinking.

"So," I continued, "the mission office in Germany decided to send women instead. Deborah and I had current passports, and neither of us had applied for visas to the East before. We could travel less noticeably on student visas. So we decided on a Tuesday afternoon that we would go. By Friday of that week we were in Vienna applying for our visas. We planned to drive all the way to Kiev with the Bibles."

"But you only reached Czechoslovakia," Sergei said.

"That's right." I was amazed that Sergei knew so many of the details. I guessed that our exploit was an urban legend within the mission. I never knew because I returned to the States a few weeks after the trip and didn't do a good job of keeping in contact with Deborah or any of the other people at the mission after I married.

"We made it through the first Eastern European border into Czechoslovakia without any problems. The guards weren't used to seeing young women driving a large vehicle into their country, so they acted kind of flirty with us. We flirted back, and they let us go right in." With a quirky awkwardness I added, "Shows you what Girl Power can do."

Neither Sue nor Sergei responded to my poor joke. I immediately felt foolish. "It wasn't Girl Power," I said quickly. "I'm sorry I said that. It was God Power all the way."

Tumbling back into the account, I summarized the rest of my story for Sue. "Deborah and I drove across Czechoslovakia and connected with our underground contact in a small town on the Polish border. He told us it wouldn't be safe to continue on to Kiev since the contact there recently had been questioned by the KGB and was now under surveillance."

I swallowed as I remembered for the first time in such a long time the humility of the older man who was our contact in Czechoslovakia. "At great risk to himself, the contact in Czechoslovakia took all of the Bibles from us. We unloaded them late at night in a…" I still couldn't bring myself to disclose specific locations so I just said, "We helped him hide them in a safe place. Then Deborah and I drove back to Germany. We were detained at the border and questioned, but our guard was distracted, and he let us go through."

"You could have gone to prison for two years if you had been caught," Sergei said.

"Yes, I know. But we weren't caught. I always thought we had it easy. The hard task was for the dozens of brave believers in Czechoslovakia. They risked imprisonment by transporting the Russian Bibles on to Kiev."

"Two of them were found out," Sergei said.

I paused. "Did they go to prison?"

"Yes."

An overwhelming sadness came over me. "What about the underground contact in Kiev? He was the one most at risk. Do you know what happened to him?"

Sergei looked down at his hands.

I turned to Sue and explained, "There was only one contact in all of Western Russia at that time who was willing to work with the mission and to receive such a large shipment of Bibles. I never found out what happened to him."

"He is well," Sergei said quietly.

I leaned forward. "Do you know him?"

Sergei looked up at me with an uncomfortable expression. "Yes, I know him. I know him too well."

Sue blinked away her stunned expression, and in a reverent whisper, she said, "Sergei, it was you, wasn't it? You were the underground contact in Kiev."

Fifteen

Sergei's humble expression told Sue and me the obvious answer that had eluded me as I was caught up in telling my side of the story.

"Yes," he said. "I was the contact in Kiev."

"Sergei," I said in a half-whisper. Now I was the one who couldn't speak.

"And you, Jenna," Sue said, now that she had found her voice, "you never told anyone, did you? Jack doesn't know this, does he?"

I shook my head.

"Why not?"

"Because the borders were closed for so many years after I came home. I didn't want to jeopardize the safety of any of the believers by giving out information that might somehow reach the wrong people."

"Thank you." Sergei was visibly moved. "Thank you for thinking of what was best for me and others like me for all these years. If you had told people what you did, you could have been a hero in America."

"No, not a hero." I almost laughed. "Sergei, you're the one who risked everything, not me."

"Sweet peaches, Jenna!" Sue blurted out. "Did you not hear yourself just tell how the Bibles got through the Czechoslovakian border? If you and Deborah hadn't done your part, then Sergei wouldn't have been able to do his."

I ignored her statement and focused on Sergei. "How did you manage to receive all the Bibles?"

He gave a concealing sort of grin. He still wasn't telling after all these years either.

"I will tell you one piece of information I think you will find interesting. I waited sixteen months for the signal that the Bibles had gotten through. When at last they came, a rumor had it that two women managed to accomplish what a dozen men were unable to do. I told the Lord I wanted one day to find a way to say thank you to the two women."

He nodded his head in a firm gesture of satisfaction. "And here you are. And here I am. And so I can tell you face-to-face what I thought I would not be able to say until I met you in heaven. Thank you, Jenna."

Sue dabbed at the tears on her face. "I can't believe this is happening."

I teared up but couldn't speak. It took me a moment before I could say, "I hope you get to meet Deborah one day, Sergei. I know you will in heaven, like you said, but I wish…"

Sergei grinned. "I know where Deborah is. I found her."

"You did?"

"Yes. When I had an opportunity many years ago, I traveled to Germany. I went to the mission office where Deborah still was working and…"

Sue and I waited for him to explain why his mouth was curling up in such a funny expression.

"I married her," Sergei said simply.

I laughed with the merriest heart ever. In the other room, our convalescing bird began to chirp madly.

Sue was still wiping tears from her cheeks. She looked like she didn't know whether to laugh or cry some more. "I can't believe this. I just can't believe it. I mean, I can believe it. I do believe y'all are both telling the truth. It's just amazing. That's what it is: truly amazing."

Sue and I didn't make it to Murano that day. As it was, we barely had the main meal ready for the returning band of brothers at noon. We sat at the dining room table for several hours talking with Sergei. We heard more about Deborah and all the work the two of them did for the mission now. We saw pictures of their two children and heard a few sparse details about what Sergei's life had been like during the Soviet years.

When the others returned from San Giorgio Maggiore, a few of them joined us at the dining room table and told us about their experience at morning worship. One of the Benedictine monks who spoke English offered to give them a tour of the facilities. Fikret especially appreciated the behind-the-scenes tour. He said it was time well spent.

Sergei and I kept quiet with the others about our time well spent. My mind was still wrapping itself around the extraordinary experience of meeting Sergei and comparing our stories. In an odd way, the event was so amazing that it felt funny trying to talk about it. Almost as if no one would believe us.

I knew that wasn't true, but I had so much to process. Sergei had taken me back to a place in my heart and mind that I hadn't visited in a long time.

Sue seemed to understand instinctively, and she respected my somber contemplations.

After lunch the men decided to take some free time and change their last group strategy meeting to that evening. Right away, four of them began discussing a visit to the museum with the Tintoretto paintings that Marcos had so highly recommended the night before.

Eduardo invited Sue and me to go with them.

"I'm going to stay here," I said, without offering an explanation.

Sue provided one for me. "She has had an unusually

full morning. But I would love to go with y'all. When are you leaving?"

The art enthusiasts departed in a cluster, with Sue, her map, and her guidebook as their guiding light. I knew they would appreciate her directional skills, and she would enjoy being with them.

Sergei was one of the men who stayed back at the apartment. He called home and invited me to say hello to Deborah. We spoke for several minutes. It was a sweet yet clumsy sort of conversation. The best part was that she and I were reconnected. Living now as we did, in a world of global cell phones and e-mails, I knew we could stay connected easily.

When I hung up, Sergei asked if I would please tell Sam about our tandem history. We went looking for Sam and found him on the narrow balcony off the princess bedroom. Pulling two more chairs out into the fresh air, we talked while small boats floated down the canal below us.

Sam took in our story with a steady smile and nodded his head. "This certainly explains why your name kept coming to mind when we pulled the details together for this retreat. Now I know why. Clearly you needed to be here for something more than stirring spaghetti sauce."

I smiled.

"I'm beginning to think that 90 percent of what we should be doing as believers is just to show up," Sam said.

"God's Spirit takes it from there. I'm glad you showed up this week, Jenna."

"And I'm glad you showed up all those years ago in Czechoslovakia," Sergei added.

I looked down at my hands. Now I was the one who had nibbled off two of her fingernails since breakfast. "To be honest, the main reason I agreed to come on this trip was because I thought it would be good for Sue. She needed a break." I told them briefly about Jack's car accident and what the past few years had been like for my sister-in-law.

"I wouldn't have guessed she had gone through so much," Sergei said.

"Interesting, isn't it?" Sam spun his gold band around his finger, as he looked down at the canal and contemplated aloud. I could remember watching him twist that same wedding ring around his finger all those years ago when we sat at a table talking after meals in Austria. His familiar little habit was somehow comforting to me in the midst of all the tumbling thoughts of the day.

"It's so easy for us to make assumptions about people," Sam went on. "We need to tell each other our stories. We need to be heard, and we need to hear ourselves." He looked at me over the top rim of his glasses. "I would like to hear your story, Jenna. What happened after you left Europe that summer?"

I didn't feel as if Sam were putting me on the spot to

divulge my entire personal history. Rather I felt an invitation had been extended. An invitation simply to tell my story. For some reason that was different than launching into a confession of a long series of life choices.

I drew in a clarifying breath of warm afternoon air. "Three significant experiences happened to me since I last saw you. I married, I had a daughter, and I divorced."

The telling of my story was brief. It was humbling and at the same time liberating to tell both these men about how I returned to Minnesota at the age of twenty-two, ready to take on the world. I intended to return to Europe to work full-time with the same ministry Sergei now headed. But then I met Gerry. I made an impulsive decision and married him right away. We had two rough years together before Callie was born. Our daughter was only three months old when Gerry moved in with his long-time girlfriend. They had had a child together before I met Gerry, but I didn't know that at the time. I fought the divorce. I fasted and prayed. But when Gerry and his girlfriend were expecting their second child, I finally signed the divorce papers. I was twenty-six years old, and nothing during that intense season of my life had gone the way I had thought it would.

To my surprise, neither of the men changed expressions during the telling of my story. Neither of them appeared to judge me. I was met with acceptance and understanding. I couldn't remember feeling that way before whenever I'd talked about my past.

The sensation that washed over me in the afternoon sunlight was, *So this is what grace feels like.*

I don't think I had ever felt I had been shown grace before. Now I knew grace was being extended to me. What made it different this time was that I was ready to reach out and take hold of the grace being offered.

"And here you are," Sam said.

"Yes, here I am." I felt new. I felt absolved and free. Unshackled. The shame was off me. I can't explain how it happened, but the shame was off, and the grace was on.

"So, Jenna," Sam said, "I have a question for you. What is the Lord asking you to do now?"

"I honestly don't know." I looked at Sergei and then back at Sam. Both of them seemed attentive to my response.

"All I know is that I'm in a new season. A time of beginnings. I'm available. I just don't know what I'm supposed to do."

Sam looked at me and said, "Feed His lambs, Jenna."

"Yes," Sergei immediately agreed. "Feed His sheep."

They popped out their admonitions so quickly and in sync that it seemed they had practiced the lines ahead of time. I could tell they hadn't premeditated their words, though, by the way they turned to each other with mutual looks of surprise.

"Do you see how much you have to offer to so many women?" Sam asked.

I shook my head. What did I have to offer? I didn't do

anything particularly well. I couldn't play the piano or sing like Sue. I wasn't a teacher. I'd never been told I was a good counselor. Or a good cook. Or a good anything, for that matter.

Truth be told, I didn't know what my spiritual gift was. A year ago a woman at church asked if I wanted to take a spiritual gift test. I declined. I secretly was afraid I would flunk the test. The policy at our church already limited areas where I could serve because I was divorced. If I flunked a spiritual gift test, they really wouldn't know what to do with me.

"I'm not sure how I can help other women."

"Jenna, don't you see how God has uniquely prepared you?" Sam asked. "You have been to dark places. You know what it is to lose hope. You know what it is to live with something you cannot change. Yet you have taken grace and filled your life with it. Now you have more than enough to give others."

I still didn't know how those attributes could benefit other women.

"You are a courier, Jenna," Sergei added with one of his near-grins that seemed to slip through his teeth and press his lips upward. "You can now smuggle truth and hope into places where it has not been for a long time."

"How?"

"Show up," Sam said with a gleam in his eyes.

I remembered every word those two men spoke over

me on that balcony. I'm sure I will remember every word for the rest of my life. They blessed me and empowered me to "go," even though I still didn't know where I was supposed to go or exactly what I was supposed to do.

The beautiful part was that I didn't need to know those specifics yet. What I did know was that I was free. I, at long last, had put on the grace God had given me. It was real. Very real. And I had a feeling it looked even better on me than my swishy new skirt.

When the three of us finally came in from the balcony, I went to the kitchen to check on Netareena, as I had promised Sue I would. The eagerly chirping bird ruffled her feathers and tried to leave the confining box. Everything in me wanted to scoop her up and hold her out the open window and say, "Fly! Be free!" But she wasn't quite ready.

I made sure she had more water and bread crumbs, and I whispered, "Almost, Netareena. Keep getting stronger. You'll fly soon."

At five o'clock that evening, the art club returned. They were weary but talkative about the wonders they had seen that day. Sue and I could have launched into a deep, long conversation; we had many things to discuss. Instead we spent what was left of the day pouring ourselves into cooking and organizing. A sweet peace covered us. It had been a good day.

It struck me, as I pulled my nightclothes out of my

suitcase, that perhaps 90 percent of what a woman is supposed to do when she enters the next season of life is to simply "show up." If she can do that without packing a lot of shame, regret, or guilt into her baggage, it certainly makes for a lighter, more liberating, and enjoyable journey.

When Sue and I retreated to our rooftop loft, she brought the bird with her in its cushy box. I told Sue I thought Netareena would be ready to fly away soon. I expected her to make an attempt once we got her up on the open rooftop.

Instead, she nested down in her waxed green bean box for the night. Sue and I followed her lead and got comfy.

"Tell me about the museum this afternoon," I said.

"It was amazing. But before I tell you about it, we need to talk about something else."

"Okay."

"Jenna, I need to apologize to you."

"For what?"

"I need to apologize for judging you."

"Judging me? For what?"

"For being divorced."

"Oh."

"Jenna, I'm sorry. We lost so many years when we would have been close like we are now. I never gave you a chance. I judged you wrongly."

"It's okay, Sue. Really. It's all in the past."

"I know, but I realized something today. When my life and Jack's life went into what I guess you could call a 'valley of the shadow of death,' you came close to us. You weren't afraid. I mean, you even moved to Dallas."

"That was different. I moved to Dallas because I could. I had space in my life to do that. I wanted to be near you guys."

"I know. And I'm so glad you came. I don't know what I would have done without you. The thing is, when you went through your worst 'valley of the shadow' time all those years ago, I wasn't there for you. I never was there for Callie."

"Oh, Sue, you don't have to go back there and blame yourself for anything."

She propped herself up on an elbow and looked at me. "I just want to say I'm sorry, Jenna. I'm sorry I wasn't there for you. That was wrong of me."

My sister-in-law's honest words, spoken under the watchful eyes of the Venetian stars, were like fragrant, healing oil poured out over that painful season of my life. She had no idea how her loving apology covered all the snubbing I had received from so many others. "Sue—"

"I know what you're going to say now. You're going to say 'shame off me,' and you're right. The shame is off me now that I told you. I just had to say it."

"Actually, I was going to say something else." I leaned closer. "Grace on you, Sue."

She took it, smiled, and lay back down. "Grace on you, too, Jenna."

"Yes," I echoed. "Grace on both of us."

Sixteen

$\mathcal{S}$ome *nights in my life* I have slept for ten hours and not dreamed at all. I've awakened from those nights exhausted and restless.

But that night in Venice, when Sue and I fell asleep under a blanket of grace, I slept for only four hours. However, I dreamed the whole night. I dreamed while staring at the stars, I dreamed while watching the moon rise with a fuller-lipped smile than the one she wore the night we arrived. I dreamed in whispers as I prayed. I dreamed in my sleep. And I woke refreshed and energized.

Sue woke in her usual, "How can it be morning already?" mode, but then she remembered the little bird. "How are you today, little one? Any better? Are you hungry?"

The bread crumbs Sue had left in the nest the night before appeared untouched.

"She's still breathing." Sue leaned close but didn't touch the bird so as not to frighten it.

"Give her another day," I suggested. "She might be building up her strength by sleeping a lot."

"Today is the last day the men are here, right?"

"Yes. I told Sam we would prepare a large breakfast before they all left. We should get going to the panetteria."

"I'll go with you," Sue said. "Maybe the gondolier will be back today, and I can watch him flirt with you."

"Don't count on it."

My words turned out prophetic. No gondoliers lined up at the bakery.

Lucia cheerfully greeted us and held up a round loaf of bread with a nice brown crust.

"Si," I said, not knowing what type of bread it was but feeling confident it would be delicious. We bought nearly as much bread as we had the day before since the men had eaten every crumb.

I paid Lucia and wished I knew how to tell her that this was the last day we would be buying for an army. Piecing together an awkward sentence with the few Italian words I knew, I said to Lucia, "Domani, solo due. No nove. Si? Solo due."

Lucia nodded and said "ciao." I hoped she understood because I didn't want her to fire up the oven the next day for an extra large batch of daily bread.

Sue and I took off once again looking like the neighborhood bakery bandits, our shopping bags stuffed to overflowing.

A block away we were greeted by an aging Italian woman wearing a scarf over her head and pulling a wheeled shopping tote. Inside the squeaky-wheeled shopping tote was a stuffed gunnysack tied at the top with rope. She stopped walking and eyed Sue and me expectantly.

"*Uvas?*" she asked.

Sue and I smiled and nodded slightly in an attempt to be polite. She seemed too nicely groomed to be a beggar. We would have gone around her, but she was blocking the walkway.

"Due?" She tilted her head and added a string of other Italian words.

We recognized the Italian word for "two," and I nodded again that, yes, there were two of us.

"Are you tracking with this woman?" Sue asked.

"Not yet."

"Due uvas?" she asked.

I tentatively said, "Si?"

The woman responded with a look of satisfaction and a nod.

"Does she want money?" Sue asked.

"I don't think so."

The woman reached into the gunnysack and the bundle of something inside rustled around. Sue and I exchanged confused expressions and took a step back. The sound of a chicken cackling caused us to reach for each other at the same time and nearly drop our shopping bags bulging with bread.

"Ah!" The woman extracted her hand and jubilantly offered us an undeniably fresh egg. She placed it in Sue's hand.

Sue looked as stunned as I felt. "Jenna, it's still warm. Creepy warm."

"Don't drop it, whatever you do," I muttered back to her.

"What am I supposed to do with it?"

"Just hold it and keep smiling."

The woman again reached into her bag of chicken tricks, and with only a funny squawk to once again prepare us for the glad event, another warm brown egg magically appeared. This one was handed to me.

"I think I'm supposed to pay her," I said, not sure how I was going to pull out my wallet while juggling the bags of bread and the fresh egg.

"Here," I said to Sue, rolling the egg into her hand, as if we were playing some sort of mixer game. "Hold this for me, will you?"

"Jenna!"

"Hang on." I put down one of the bags of bread and pulled out some coins. I had no idea what the going street value was in Venice for two hot eggs.

The woman was now fiddling with a cardboard box

under the wiggling gunnysack. She lifted up the box to me and opened the lid, as if seeking my approval for the contents.

The box contained more eggs. At least twenty. All brown and stacked neatly so as not to break.

Sue peered into the box. "Maybe the *due* meant two dozen and not just two eggs. Maybe the two I'm holding are just the samples to prove her eggs are fresh."

"A baker's dozen?" I speculated. "Or should I say a baker's two dozen? Is that what I agreed to buy?"

The woman was watching us converse, waiting for me to take the two dozen eggs. As soon as I took the box, she held out her hand for her payment.

I gave her all the coins I had. She flipped through them with her thumb and appeared satisfied with the amount I handed her. Business transaction satisfactorily completed, she bid us a buon giorno, turned, and made her way down the cobblestones with the poor, clandestine chicken being jostled in her hideaway gunnysack.

Sue and I stood there watching her go.

Glancing down at the two brown eggs in her hand, Sue asked, "I don't know if I'm supposed to take these home to hatch or scramble them up with a little cheese and fresh basil."

"I would advise against the hatching option," I said. "Our Fine Feathered Friends Convalescent Ward is occupied at the moment."

"What are we going to do with all these eggs? We already have enough for omelets."

"We'll think of something." I juggled everything and picked up the pace. "We need to start breakfast for the men before they have to leave!"

Sue and I entered the apartment as the men were singing the same hymn we had heard them sing their first morning together. We had missed Malachi's devotional reading of the Scriptures again, and I was sad about that. Sad and grumpy. If we hadn't dawdled with the crazy egg lady, we might have been back in time.

Kicking into high gear, Sue and I went to work in the kitchen. Instead of making individual omelets, we threw all our prepared ingredients into our three frying pans along with the eggs we had in the refrigerator. The scrambled eggs were ready the same time the coffee was. Sue and I hurried to finish our preparations for the Last Breakfast, as we were now calling it.

I went into the dining room and placed the dishes around the table, adjusting each place setting to just the right angle for the accompanying chair. I used linen napkins and folded one in a triangle on top of each china plate. I wanted this meal to be nice for these men.

The uneven floor made me smile as I moved around behind the table. Who had dined in this room in the ages past? Who had served them? Who were the people who had put their feet beneath this table, and what had happened to them? Did they ever gather in the large sitting room to pray, as these men were doing now? Or did they gather there only in the evenings while a string quartet played Vivaldi?

This was a special place. And these past few days had been special. Even if diabolical deeds had been done at one time under this roof, I firmly believed the invisible territories had been reclaimed through worship and the reading of God's Word that had echoed off the high ceilings the past few days.

I poured grape juice into each of the crystal glasses. From the other room I could hear the men conversing with each other after their morning prayers. They were affirming each other, encouraging each other, and blessing each other's ministries. This wasn't a meeting of competitors. I felt as if I had been in the company of mighty warriors for the kingdom of God. These men were going from this sacred place today as a united group, ready to do damage to the kingdom of darkness.

I breathed in deeply the same way I'd breathed when Marcos told us about the gold that disappeared from the Ca'd'Oro. Now I wasn't hoping to breathe in gold. I wanted to absorb one of the many blessings being passed around in the adjoining room.

Just as Sue and I finished dishing up the food, the men entered the dining room. The table was ready and waiting for them. The fresh bread was on a cutting board in the middle of the table. Each plate had been served with a generous portion of the steaming scrambled eggs. Sue and I paused before entering the kitchen, making sure the salt and pepper were on the table as well as milk and sugar for the coffee.

Nodding to each other that all the essentials were covered, we turned to go into the kitchen. But Malachi stopped us by meeting our gaze and motioning for us to pause. We waited for him to indicate what was missing. He motioned for both of us to come over to the table.

"What can we get for you?"

"Two more plates of eggs, please. And two more forks. And two more glasses."

We returned to the kitchen to fetch the two plates of eggs Sue and I had scooped for ourselves. We didn't mind giving up our breakfast. It just seemed odd.

"We can make some more," Sue said to me. "We have plenty of eggs, that's for sure."

"But why does he want these? Is someone coming we didn't know about?"

She shrugged. I followed her into the dining room with two more crystal goblets, linen napkins, and two sets of silverware.

Malachi had made room on either side of him for the two extra plates. I set up the silverware, napkins, and goblets. The other men looked up. Apparently they didn't know what Malachi was doing, either.

"Please." He rose from his chair and held out an open palm to Sue and me. "Come and eat breakfast."

The conversations were silenced, as all eyes turned to Sue and me. Sergei rose and went to the corner of the room where several extra chairs were lined up against the wall. He brought two of them over to the table, as the others made more room for us.

Sue shot me a look of subdued astonishment. It took me a moment before I remembered that those were the words she and I had read yesterday morning from John 21. Jesus had invited His disciples to come and have breakfast with Him. Now Malachi and the other men were extending such an invitation to Sue and me.

We took our seats quietly. Extravagant hospitality can certainly catch a person off guard. I felt as if I had stepped into a painting that we had seen at the Accademia. Like the women in that painting, we were unexpected subjects in a familiar composition. The original title of the huge art piece had been *The Last Supper.* The title was changed to "The Feast of the House of Levi" because the artist had included so many people around the table who weren't present in the biblical account of the Last Supper. Like one of the subjects in that painting, I felt that I didn't belong here. And yet I'd been welcomed to come and dine as an equal.

Sam passed the loaf of bread to me. I broke off a portion and took a bite. I reached for the glass of grape juice

Malachi had filled for me, pouring from his own glass. I took a sip and recognized the elements, the combination of tastes in my mouth, the sensation in my spirit. Without orchestrating it, we were gathered together in the name of Christ and breaking bread in remembrance of Him. Communion. A table where all are welcome. Even me.

The moment pressed itself into the eternal part of my spirit. I still carry it there.

I took a bite of the scrambled eggs. Immediately I knew what to do with the double dozen we had purchased from the gunnysack lady.

An hour later, as Sue and I were finishing up in the kitchen, the sound of luggage wheels rolling over the marble floors echoed around us. All of those suitcases were heading for the front door.

I was wiping the last of the dishes and had a knife in my hand when Sergei stepped into the kitchen. He raised an eyebrow, and I quickly put down the knife with a chuckle just begging to leak out.

"Please give my love to Deborah and your children. Tell her I will e-mail as soon as I get home."

"I will. Would you mind if I took a picture of both of you? For Deborah. She asked."

Sue and I looped our arms around each other's shoulders and turned toward the camera.

"Is my hair a fright?" Sue asked.

I don't know why she only asked that question when

picture-taking was involved. Certainly she had to know that her hair almost always was a little disheveled, a little on the fright-side of the measuring stick.

"You look fabulous," I said, without turning away from Sergei's camera and keeping my grin fixed. It was my signal to him to hurry up and take the picture before Sue started fussing with her lobster locks.

"Oh, who cares," Sue said. We froze our pose together beside a stack of pots and pans.

I felt so happy. It made little sense. Such simple moments didn't usually overwhelm me with such a feeling of pure delight. But my emotions were off-the-chart elevated. Nothing this day had been simple or common. Everything around us felt sacred. Even these pots and pans and the yellow apron I wore with stains from the sauces I'd prepared. I felt like I was now the Italian mama welcoming and sending away visitors with hugs and tears and doing it in such a way that the scent of garlic and onions lingered long after the guests were out of the kitchen.

"I have a favor to ask." Sergei put away his camera.

"If you're going to ask if y'all can have some sandwiches to take with you on the train, we already made them, and they're waiting on the table by the front door."

"Thank you. But I was not going to ask about sandwiches. I wanted to ask if you would consider something. I know this is a very big favor."

"That's okay," Sue said. "What is it?"

"Would you consider coming to Kiev sometime to take my wife out laughing?"

I loved the way he said "take my wife out laughing," as if that were something women did naturally, just as young lovers go out dancing and lonely men go out drinking.

"Yes," was my immediate answer.

"Take your wife where?" Sue asked.

"Out laughing," I repeated. "We would love to come to Kiev and take Deborah out laughing, Sergei."

Sergei looked pleased. "This is good. You, both of you, coming to see her. Yes, this would be good medicine."

"Are you saying you want me to come, too?" Sue asked.

"Of course. The two of you are a team, are you not?"

Sue looked to me, and I put my arm around her shoulder again, even though we already had posed for the picture. I looked at Sue with admiration. "Yes, we're a team."

"This will mean very much to Deborah. And to me. I believe that you, both of you, can give to my wife what I cannot give her, as much as I have hoped and tried."

Sue jutted out her chin. "No offense, but that's because you're a man. Laughing is a job for a couple of Sisterchicks."

"That's right," I said. "You tell Deborah that the Sisterchicks will be coming her way."

Sergei looked amused now. "Okay, I will tell Deborah the superchicks are coming one day to visit."

"No, not superchicks. Sisterchicks," Sue corrected him.

"Neither of us is very 'super,'" I said. "But we are sisters."

Sergei liked that. He stepped forward, and both of us took a step forward. He hugged us firmly while issuing a succession of Russian words over the top of our heads. I didn't have to ask what he was saying. I knew he was blessing us. And I took it.

"Grace on you, brother," I murmured in return. "May goodness and mercy follow you all the days of your life."

He nodded, accepting my attempt at a blessing, and left the kitchen with one of his cautious grins trapped behind his teeth and barely leaking out.

As soon as I was sure he was all the way out of the kitchen, I pressed a big, smacky kiss into the palm of my hand and tossed it after him.

"What was that?" Sue asked.

"That was a big fat baci."

She paused as if trying to remember what a baci was. "Well, you better watch what you're throwing at that kitchen door."

"Oh, this from the woman who nearly used that same door for a knife-throwing contest yesterday!"

Sue gave me a wild look of mock indignation. "I told you it was a butter knife."

"Sisters?" Came a deep voice from just inside the door. Malachi was standing back, seeming to assess the situation before entering through the door that was the topic of our banter.

Sue and I both laughed, and Malachi looked relieved. "I have come to say farewell to you both." He held up his large hands, with the palms toward us, and said, "May the peace of Christ be upon you."

"And also with you," I said.

"We have something for you." Sue went to the side counter and picked up a box containing twenty-six well-packed hard-boiled eggs. More than double what Malachi had arrived with.

"An offering for your wife," I said. "We were blessed with more than we could use."

Malachi didn't say anything. He didn't need to.

Seventeen

It was over. The retreat had ended, and all the men had filed out with their luggage. The front door closed behind them, leaving Sue and me alone in the huge palace apartment.

"You should have married a missions director," Sue said. Then catching herself, she froze and said, "I didn't mean…"

"I know what you meant; you don't have to explain. It's okay." I hesitated and then confessed, "I've thought the same thing more than once. And you know what? The reality is, I didn't marry a missions director. I didn't do a lot of things. But this is my life now, and I've begun to realize that I have options. Lots of options."

"Like going to Kiev someday."

"Yes, like going to Kiev someday."

"You know what?" Sue said as we walked back to the kitchen. "I'm going to miss those guys."

She and I didn't have anything particularly urgent to do in the kitchen. It just had become instinctive for us to go there.

Sue sighed. "When the men first arrived, I couldn't wait for them to leave so you and I could come up with our own schedule and not have to sleep on the roof. Now I wish they weren't leaving."

She and I probably would have broken down into a full-on melancholy fest, but we both spotted something that captured our attention. Netareena was out of her nest and hopping around on the kitchen floor.

"Look at you! You're up and around. What do you think, Jenna? Should we take her to the window and let her go?" Sue asked.

"I don't know. Is she ready to fly? Or is she only able to hop?"

Sue leaned down to scoop up the bird, and it took flight. Her wings only carried her about four inches off the ground before she came back down peeping loudly.

"You poor little thing!" Sue reached for the bird again. This time her motions were quicker, and the bird didn't have as much strength to resist. Sue carefully tucked Netareena in her nest-box. "What do you suppose we can do for her?"

"Keep feeding her. See what happens. She's almost all the way there."

We made sure the nest was in a protected location on the kitchen floor and gave Netareena more water and bread crumbs. Then we set to work cleaning up the apartment before the heat of the afternoon poured through the front windows. Sue and I only had the rest of today and the next day to fit in our sightseeing.

I thought about that as we gathered the piles of sheets we stripped from the beds and bundled by each bedroom door. Sue had spent much more time with the tour book than I had, but I knew I better speak up if I wanted to see any particular sights.

We still hadn't seen the main tourist area of the Piazza San Marco. I was interested in going inside the Basilica of San Marco. The island of Murano still appealed to me as well. But I didn't feel I had to see any of it. This week already had been so full of every good thing; what more could I ask for?

The truth was, as much as I was enjoying Venice, I could have gone home right then and felt as if I'd seen enough to last me for a lifetime.

Sue and I worked together quickly, remaking the beds, opening the shuttered windows wide to let in the last of the morning breeze, and straightening up each of the rooms. The princess suite was our last room to clean. It didn't take long. We collected our luggage from where we had stored it in the broom closet and moved our things into the spacious room.

Sue sat down at the piano and played a hauntingly lovely song. "Do you want to hear something really crazy?" she asked between the long notes.

"Are you going to say you still want to sleep on the roof?"

"No. Why? Is that what you want to do?"

"I was thinking about it. But we've waited for our chance to stay here in the princess suite. Even though it's only for two nights, I suppose we should enjoy the luxury while we can."

"I agree."

"What were you going to say? You asked if I wanted to hear something really crazy."

"I forgot what I was going to say." Sue kept playing.

I went out on the balcony and made myself comfortable, putting up my feet on one of the chairs. It was just about time for one of my little naps. A "nappini" would have been a good name for my Italian siestas. Closing my eyes, I leaned my head back and listened to Sue play a beautiful piece that contained all the high notes. The music sounded fragile.

Ten minutes into my peaceful snooze, after the sun had sufficiently warmed my shoulders so that all my muscles were like linguine, Sue came out on the balcony and stood next to me. I could feel her presence before I actually cracked open one eye and looked at her. She was gazing down on the canal, humming to herself.

I wished I had my camera. I was sure my brother would love to have a picture of Sue's profile as I saw it at that moment. He wouldn't have seen this pose for a long time. I would entitle it "Sue at Peace."

But the more I studied her through my one eye, opened just a slit, the more I realized her outward appearance was at peace, but her countenance had an invisible butter knife raised over it. She was at peace, yet ready to go to war at the same time.

"Are you awake?" Sue asked in a low voice without turning to look at me.

"Maybe."

"Do you want to go do something?"

"Maybe."

"I have several suggestions of what we could do with the rest of the day."

"And do any of those suggestions involve gelato?"

"Maybe." Sue turned the tables on my sly answer.

I told her to lead the way, and she did—all the way to the Fondamenta Nuove along the lagoon waterfront. We waited for a vaporetto to take us to the island of Murano.

Only a few other people joined us when we boarded the vaporetto. Several tourists were already on the water-bus when it picked us up. We rode across the moody water, with sea spray dotting our faces and clinging to the surface of our clothes.

Signs made it easy for us to figure out where to go to see the glassblowers. We entered what looked like an old barn and found several glassblowers at work behind a metal railing. Other visitors shuffled into the small viewing space along with us, and we stood there watching these craftsmen the way people line up at the zoo to watch the lions in their unnatural environment. It felt inhuman to me for these men to be on display, yet at the same time what they were doing was fascinating, and I was glad we could watch.

A young, dynamic man stood at the railing with a glassblown fishbowl in his arms that obviously was for tips. He gave a brief description of the ancient method of heating the sand mixture to such a high temperature that the sand melts. Long metal poles then are inserted in the melted goo and come out looking like a lollipop on a long stick. The poles are turned evenly as the glass cools.

Then the amazing part happens. The artisans blow through the end of the metal pipe, and the air expands the glass ball to whatever shape the men are trying to achieve.

It all happens rapidly, with quick turns of the pole or pipe. Metal tongs are used to shape handles on pitchers while the glass is still white-hot. Delicate stems on crystal goblets take less than a few seconds to shape.

Our guide presented the information in three languages: English, German, and French. He asked if we had any questions and held out the tip jar with a wide grin. Sue found some tip money and covered the "free" admission for both of us. I wanted to stay and watch two artisans work together on what looked like it would become a large serving bowl. But we were asked to file out through the doors and into the gift shop where rows and rows of glass shelves displayed every sort of glass figurine as well as every useful glass item known to humanity.

I was drawn to the light fixtures hanging overhead. They were like the chandeliers at the palace apartment, intricate with various colors and shapes to form the amazing designs.

"Sue, look at these. Can you see the price tag? How much are these?"

She tried to turn her head just right to see the hanging tag. "I'm not sure. Should we ask someone?"

"Let's see if this one is marked more clearly." I moved to the back of the store. "It's smaller but looks like the same style as the one above our dining room table. Can you read this tag?"

"It says four thousand," Sue said.

"Four thousand euros?"

"That's right," a soft-spoken salesman said, coming up alongside Sue and me. "We pay for the shipping. We have wall sconces that go with this one."

We both were surprised to receive such a smooth sales

pitch in perfect English and took a moment to respond. In our hesitation, he made a second pitch.

"Our nicer works are for viewing in the private gallery. Would you like to follow me?"

Sue and I looked at each other with expressions that seemed to say, "I'm in if you're in," and off we went, following this stranger up three steps and through a door that led into a beautiful, modern display room. We saw other visitors with salesmen, some speaking French, others English, but all of them seemed to be in the midst of haggling over a particular item.

"This way, please." We followed across the carpeted floor and into a separate room that contained a dozen hanging glass chandeliers. Each of them was a work of art.

"Sweet peaches," Sue said under her breath.

The light glimmered around the room through all the colors and glass reflections, creating an otherworldly ambience. If ever there was a place where fairies went to dance, this was it.

"I believe you were interested in this particular style?" he pointed to an extravagant piece that came with an equally extravagant price tag. It was the twin of the one hanging in the dining room.

"We should tell you that we aren't in a position to purchase any of your beautiful fixtures." I hoped we weren't going to be thrown out on our ears.

He nodded graciously. "You are welcome to look around. Tell me if I can help."

"Thank you."

He left us in the fairy ballroom, and Sue and I stood in silent marvel over all the color and shining diamonds of light that fell on us.

"I've never seen anything like this," Sue said.

"Me neither. And just think, the place we're staying at has at least four of these hanging fixtures."

"And don't forget all the matching wall sconces."

"The light fixtures alone at the palace apartment must be worth twenty-five or thirty thousand euros."

"I feel like we should buy something," Sue said.

"I think that's what they're hoping, but what can we afford?"

"I don't know. Let's look around."

Sue and I prowled with great caution. We didn't see any "You break it, you bought it" signs, but we had a feeling the policy was in effect nonetheless. After careful searching, Sue found a bowl she loved and hoped she could afford. Our salesman magically reappeared and suggested the price. It was equivalent to about eight hundred dollars.

"Sorry," Sue said. "I'll have a look in the shop downstairs. We do appreciate your assistance."

"My pleasure," he said, even though we were sure it hadn't been his pleasure.

Feeling out of place and a little nervous around all that glass, Sue and I left without buying anything and decided to explore the island. The main street that led us into the center of Murano was lined with small gift shops. Each of them carried its own variety of glassware. Several trinket items caught our attention in one store window. We entered and found the prices more within our budget.

Sue bought a glass Christmas tree with tiny colored balls of glass affixed to the ends of the branches. I found a vase that captivated me with its narrow core and fluted rim. The vase was a regal shade of purple with flowers painted on the side. The clerk wrapped it in an Italian newspaper and placed it in a paper bag, then wrapped the bag into a tight bundle and taped the edges. She seemed pleased that we appreciated the items in her store.

Walking on, we came to a large bridge that took us across a canal and over to a row of houses. The housing and the feel on this island were much simpler and smaller than the neighborhoods we had walked through in Venezia. On Murano lived fisherman and tradesman, and their lifestyle was reflected in the surroundings. Laundry hung from lines strung between two houses. Skinny dogs scouted out every corner with their tails in the air. Children held their mama's hand and looked over their shoulders at us with their big brown eyes asking what we were doing in their neighborhood.

The funny part was that Sue and I felt comfortable

there, off the beaten path, away from the tourist clusters. We stopped at a small café along the canal. Sue said she felt more at home at the café where no one spoke English than we had in the showroom where we had a personal attendant who spoke and understood English well.

Ordering was getting easier for both of us. We had a pretty good idea of what we would receive when we asked for ravioli and lasagna. The only surprise was the *malaga* gelato Sue ordered for dessert. We found out later it was a rum raisin flavor.

Sue gave it a 9.

"Really?"

"Why? What would you give it?"

"A 5. Maybe a 6."

"It's better than a 5 or a 6. This flavor is sweet and dense without being too complicated."

"It sounds like you're describing your cat," I teased.

"Hey, leave Moochie out of this."

"I'm going to tell Moochie you replaced him with a bird while you were away from home. I wonder what he'll do then."

"You're so mean."

"I know. I need another nappini."

"Come on," Sue said. "Let's start walking. We just sat too long and ate too much. Pasta has that affect, you know."

"And gelato doesn't?"

Sue ignored me and led the way on a personalized tour of more of the Murano island. She said she had studied the map before we took off, but I was beginning to doubt it when she led us down some pretty quiet alleyways. I was aware of the open windows just above our heads and kept my voice low in case some siestas were going on inside those homes.

We came out of the maze and walked along another canal where a row of lovely shade trees umbrellaed several park benches. The softest scent of sea salt mixed with firm green leaves. In a place of endless cobblestones and canal water, where green grass was as foreign as automobiles, the scent that met us was the closest touch of earth I remembered smelling in a week.

"This is what I wanted to see." Sue motioned to the right. "This is the *Santi Maria e Donato* church built in the seventh century and restored in the twelfth. I wanted to see the marble zigzag pattern used between the double-tiered arches."

I drew in one more deep breath of the green earth and tried to keep up with Sue.

She stopped and took in the view of the church. The two-story structure we were facing was a beautiful shade of wheat toast and soft rose. On the top floor and bottom floor were double white columns spaced between six alcoves.

"Look at that tile," Sue said. "And the marble pattern

between the levels. The tour book said the arches and tile work are the best example of Veneto Byzantine design. I was curious to see what that meant."

"It's impressive," I said.

We tried the front door and found it locked. A sign indicated the open hours; we had arrived during the afternoon siesta. Walking around to the shady side, we studied the archways that lined the structure.

"Stand in one of the archways," I said. "I'll take your picture. Pose like a statue."

Sue went for my suggestion and struck a pose. No one was around. She went for another pose, this one like a cupid on a lacey Valentine.

"Your turn." She took the camera from me.

I struck an Atlas pose inside the hollowed-out arch along the side of the church. The alcove was the perfect size and shape for a statue. I wondered if in years past magnificent statues had sat in these shadowed places and, if so, had they been carried off as spoils of war?

We heard people coming our way, and that put a freeze on my modeling career.

"These pictures are perfect." Sue reviewed them on the digital screen.

"Perfect for what? Who are you going to show them to?"

"Jack. He told me to take lots of pictures, and I've hardly taken any."

"So? Start snapping. Or, better yet, give me the camera,

and I'll start snapping. Jack isn't going to want to see me in a bunch of pictures. He's going to want to see you."

"Take pictures of everything then," Sue said. "All the interesting things that Jack would enjoy."

Sue didn't know what a great assignment she had given me. I never had realized how much I enjoyed taking pictures until Sue gave me full liberty with her camera that day.

Eighteen

I loved capturing Venezia's many faces and moods on camera. And I loved watching Sue as she and Venezia interacted with each other.

All I can say is that it's a good thing Sue was photogenic. It was an even better thing that her camera was digital. I took hundreds of pictures and deleted dozens. Since deleting was easy, I didn't hesitate to press the button at will.

The most interesting part for me was watching Sue transform. In front of the camera, she switched from the timid observer of her surroundings to the bold interpreter. She started seeing things around us in light of how she wanted Jack to see them and positioned herself to best take in the surroundings.

A bridge, like many that we had plodded across during the week, suddenly became a "subject" to Sue. She wanted to capture various angles and did everything but throw herself over the side and into Murano's Grand Canal in an effort to set up just the right composition.

This newfound shared hobby only fanned the flame of Sue's innate map-reading and puzzle-solving skills.

The gifting it uncovered in me was the opportunity to be "in the moment," which I loved, without being "in the spotlight," which never had been my forte. My only regret was that the camera was a still camera. Sue was so into our new roles that I wanted to catch some of her moments on a video camera.

I did capture a wonderful picture of Sue on the vaporetto during our return trip from Murano. The island of the glassblowers was in the background, and Sue's face was set, jaw forward, toward Venezia. Her expression was peaceful yet pensive, as it had been on the balcony earlier. She looked as if she were trying to figure out something.

Surprisingly, she hadn't asked once if her hair needed attention.

What I liked about the pictures was that she was looking ahead, not looking back. That might have been more symbolic for me than for Sue, but it came through in her posture and expression. Filtered sunlight made its way through the thin clouds and warmed the murky water. The lighting gave Sue's skin a luminous glow. She looked young and full of life, with the wind in her hair and a dancing smile on her turned-up lips.

As I studied the last picture on the digital screen, I told her I didn't think I'd seen that expression on her face once during the past five years. Maybe never.

Sue didn't respond to my comment. It could have been because the vaporetto was pulling into dock or because I'd embarrassed her. Regardless, it turned out to be a fantastic photo. Jack now has that picture framed and on his night-stand.

What followed the discovery of my delight in shooting pictures and Sue's delight in virtual tour guiding was an insane footstep frenzy. We felt we had to tromp all over Venice and capture everything on film.

Instead of taking our usual straight route back to the palace, Sue did a quick study of the map and led us a long way around, through a neighborhood that had beautifully restored buildings along a canal. So much of Venice was dilapidated and past due for repairs, but this area had received special attention and care. Colorful geraniums cascaded from planters on the balconies. I captured a picture of the flowers clashing with Sue's hair as she stood in the foreground.

We more or less circled Venice by foot, shooting pictures every few minutes along the way. At Sue's suggestion, we avoided San Marco Square. It was the middle of the afternoon, and if all we had heard was correct, the crowds would be at their thickest.

"We'll make tomorrow our San Marco day," Sue said.

"We'll start early and have time to take it all in."

That plan was fine with me.

We came upon a sunny piazza with a corner bookstore that looked inviting. At the outdoor café across the way, a small man was playing a large accordion while diners ate under widespread café umbrellas.

Sue and I looked through the books displayed on the table in front of the bookstore. Many of them were in English. I picked up one of the books of photographic studies of Venice. The text was printed in English along with Italian, French and German. For most of the pictures, though, a written description in four language wasn't necessary. The photos spoke for themselves.

"That's gorgeous," Sue said, looking on with me.

An aerial view of Venice made it easy to see all the canals as well as the tops of the sienna buildings.

"How much is this book?" she asked.

I turned it over so she could see the price of 20 euros. Sue thought it was a little high, so we looked through other books. Even though quite a few photography books of Venice were on the table, none of the volumes seemed to overlap. Venice wore so many masks and had so many facets that each book covered different locations. The common themes repeated in a variety of ways in each book were the gondolas and the pigeons at San Marco Square.

"We're going to have to take a gondola ride." Sue gazed at one of the pictures. She had gone back to the original book with the higher price tag. All her attention was on a picture of a craftsman who was hand-polishing a long, upside-down, black gondola balanced on a sawhorse inside a workshop.

"It says here that two hundred years ago Venice had ten thousand gondolas, but now there are less than five hundred. Each one is handmade, and they're painted black with six coats of special paint."

I quietly reached for the camera. Stepping back, I took a picture of Sue looking at the book about Venice while standing in Venice.

"Did you just take my picture?"

"Yes."

"Why? I wasn't looking."

"I know. But you're going to buy that book. I know you are. Jack is going to ask where you bought it, and now you'll be able to show him."

"You are a better salesperson than the man at the glass display room. What makes you so sure I'm going to buy this?"

"Because you're going to get home and try to tell Jack all these details like how much a gondola weighs—"

"A half a ton, it says here."

I gave Sue a pretend flustered look for the way she cut me off.

"I'm sorry. You were saying?"

"You're getting that book, Sue. And now you'll have a

picture of you looking at the book before you bought it."

She looked at it again, this time with her chin slightly elevated and her profile tilted toward the best light. "Go ahead and take another shot, then. Just in case the first one doesn't turn out."

I think it's fun to periodically support a friend's fleeting moment of vanity. We spend too much time tearing ourselves down and keeping mental lists of our flaws. When the chance comes to nurture each other's finer points, I'm all for it.

That must explain why it didn't bother me to keep taking shots of Sue as she posed this way and that. She could be strikingly photogenic when I caught her in just the right light and position.

Sue bought the book, of course, and we continued our walking tour, eyes open, camera snapping, drinking it all in. Whenever we found ourselves in a passageway thick with tourists, we went another route. Sue's sense of direction was extraordinary.

My sense of smell was what impressed Sue. I sniffed out something delectable and led us to a pizzeria where the most enticing fragrance of garlic and artichoke wafted out its open door.

We stepped inside the small, dimly lit pizzeria and saw the wood oven where the pizzas were having the garlic breath baked out of them. A couple of Italian words, a thumb and finger visual for "due," and a couple of euros bought us huge slices of flat-crusted pizza that we walked outside with to enjoy.

"How strange that there's no cheese," Sue said. "It's all tomato sauce and a garden of vegetables."

I didn't respond. I was too busy sliding the pointed end of my Italian vegetable garden into my happy mouth. "Mmm." As soon as I swallowed, I said, "A ten. Definitely a ten. Do you realize this is our first taste of Italian pizza?"

"It's okay." Sue dabbed the corner of her mouth with the back of her hand.

"Okay? Just okay?"

She nodded. "It's no tiramisu gelato."

"Therein lies the difference in our choices of comfort food. I am a bread woman rather than a sugar mama."

"That's because you're a Midwestern born-and-bred baby. I, on the other hand, was raised on sweet tea."

Sue had heard more than once how I felt about her Texas sweet tea. I called it "hummingbird brown beverage" and avoided it.

We had been walking while we ate. I think our legs were on autopilot. Across from us was a narrow canal spanned by an unusually wide bridge. The edge of the bridge was wide and low enough to sit on without fear of falling backward.

I led the way, and we sat down to finish our late afternoon snack. A lone gondolier floated down the canal in our direction, as if he had been summoned. I grabbed the camera and snapped his picture.

"Gondola?" he called out with a welcoming smile.

"No thanks," I said.

He floated on. I took a picture of his back to catch the motion of the wide ribbons fluttering from his straw hat. The sunlight sliced through a gap between the buildings and illuminated his form.

"It's remarkable the way they stand at the back of the gondolas, isn't it?" Sue said. "Do you know how they stay balanced?"

"No, but I'm guessing you know." I snapped another shot.

"I read it in this wonderful book that my sister-in-law talked me into buying."

"See? You're glad already, aren't you?"

Ignoring me, she pushed ahead with her lesson in gondola structure. "They don't have keels or rudders. The bottoms are fairly flat to move over sandbars. They're designed so the prow curves to the left. That offsets the gondolier's motion with the oar and keeps the gondola from going in circles."

I watched the gondolier's steady movements as Sue talked. He did a poetic sort of dance, a smooth and soundless waltz across the shallow waters of the glassy canal.

"The oars are curved in a special way as well," Sue continued. "The balance between the prow and the oar is what makes the gondola go straight without the gondolier's hav-ing to switch the oar from side to side with each stroke."

"Amazing."

"Do you really mean that, or are you teasing me and I just can't tell the difference anymore?"

"No, I'm serious. That is amazing." Putting down the camera I turned to Sue, who still was nibbling on her pizza. "Does it seem like I'm teasing you too much?"

"No. I like the teasing. I like the way you've been having so much fun on this trip and including me in everything. At home we're both so much more serious. I like it the way it's been."

"Me, too."

"In that case, do you want to hear one more little-known fact about gondolas?"

"Yes."

"Really really?"

"Yes, really really. Tell me."

"This piece of info is actually about the gondoliers, not the gondolas. When a gondolier dies, the license to operate a gondola is passed on to his widow."

That tidbit didn't seem spectacular, so I waited for Sue to continue.

"Don't you see? It means that the gondola trade has stayed within the same families for hundreds of years. It's like Steph was saying about Paolo's café. These gondoliers are all from long lines of gondoliers."

Again, as if on cue, another gondolier came our way and called out, "*Bella donnas*! Beautiful ladies! You are waiting for me, no? You are ready for a gondola ride."

"No thanks," I called back.

"Wait!" Sue countered, turning and facing the young man in his tight-fitting striped shirt and black pants. He used the long oar to stop the gondola and direct it to the landing located a dozen stone-carved steps down from the bridge. As he looked up at us from beneath his straw hat, I realized he was the most suave gondolier we had encountered yet.

"Si, bella donna. What is your wish? I am at your *servizio*."

I was thinking, *Oh, brother!*

Sue still was solving puzzles and collecting data. "How much do y'all charge for a gondola ride?"

"Depends. Where do you want to go?"

Sue paused, seeming uncertain.

The gondolier jumped in and made it easy for her by listing prices by the hour and the half-hour. He added some of the sights we could see in those time frames.

Sue looked at me, as if waiting for my approval to part with a whole lot of money for what I'm sure would be a memorable experience.

"Fine with me," I said. "We could split the cost and just go for half an hour."

"Okay. Good. I'm sure he's going to ask for cash. Do we have enough cash on us, or do we need to find an ATM?"

"I might still have enough." I pulled out my wallet and did a quick inventory of my diminishing euros. "If you have twenty euros on you, we should have enough."

Sue smiled at our patient gondolier and called down, "Just a minute!"

"It is not a problem, bella donna. Take all the time you need. I will wait for you."

"He's smooth," Sue muttered to me under her breath.

"No kidding."

"I have thirty euros left," Sue said. "That should be plenty." She glanced down one more time and asked, "Do y'all charge more if you sing for us on the ride?"

He cupped his hand behind his ear, as if he hadn't heard her. My guess was that he had heard but he couldn't quite understand her drawl.

"You ask him, Jenna."

I broke down the question into the key words and spoke them slowly and loudly, "What is the price if you sing?"

The young man removed his straw hat and dramatically held it over his heart. Looking up at us with a Romeo-like expression, he said, "Bella donnas, you must understand. There are gondoliers who sing and there are gondoliers who make love."

With a passionate pause he added, "I do not sing."

Nineteen

O*kay, yeah.* We didn't go for a gondola ride that evening.

Sue turned a lovely rosy shade and called out to the "romantic" gondolier something along the lines of, "You better watch your mouth, young man! Don't y'all realize we're old enough to be your mother?" She said something else about how he had a proud heritage to uphold.

We picked up our belongings and left.

I wanted to laugh so hard. Sue still was fuming, so I kept my lips together and didn't look at her. She had been hoping for a face-to-face encounter with a gondolier ever since my slightly embarrassing contact at the bakery. Now that she had a chance to see how smooth these professional tourist-pleasers could be, her opinion seemed to have changed.

By the time we returned to our apartment, her indignation was diffused, but she still wasn't ready to laugh about it the way I was.

We unlocked all the doors and found the lights on in the entry room. A note from Steph waited for us on the table.

"Hi! I'm guessing you're out having a good time. I stopped by this afternoon because my uncle asked me to do an odd favor for him. He told a friend of his that he could come by at nine o'clock tonight and pick up the two extra mattresses in the storage closet. I know it's a strange time and a strange thing to loan a friend, but welcome to the Venetian way of doing things!

"I told my uncle I'd put the mattresses down in the wooden trolley cart along the side wall on the lower level. But when I went to pull out the mattresses, I couldn't find them. Who knows where they ended up. My uncle probably loaned them to another friend and forgot all about it.

"Anyway, I just wanted you to know that when a man named Pietro shows up at nine o'clock tonight, please give him the other note on the table that I wrote in Italian. It explains that the mattresses aren't here. You don't have to do anything except hand him the note.

"I'll call later this evening to check in. You have my mobile phone number, so please call me earlier if you have any problems.

"Again, I'm so sorry for the inconvenience. I hope you're having a great time.

"Ciao,

"Steph"

Sue and I looked at each other. We wore matching "uh-oh" expressions.

"Those are the mattresses we hauled up to the roof," Sue said. "That's why she couldn't find them. What should we do?"

"I think we should take them down to the cart in the entry area," I said. "When Pietro comes at nine, we can just point to the cart and off he goes. I'll call Steph and explain why she couldn't find them."

Sue didn't appear enthusiastic about my suggestion. "That's going to be a lot of work, hauling two mattresses down three flights of stairs."

"It won't be as hard as it was to haul both of them up those narrow stairs to the roof. We'll be going downhill, with gravity on our side. Plus the marble stairs are nice and wide. I think we can do it."

Sue reluctantly agreed. We went into the kitchen so I could call Steph while Sue checked on Netareena. The nest was empty. I put down the phone's receiver.

"Do you think she managed to fly out the window?" Sue asked, looking around the kitchen to make sure Netareena wasn't perched on a counter or hiding under the table.

"There she is." I pointed through the open doorway into the dining room. She had roosted on one of the elegant glass arms of the chandelier over the table, causing the light fixture to tilt to one side.

"Oh, Netareena!" Sue hurried toward her and waved her arms. "You shouldn't be up there! Do you have any idea how much that light costs?"

Netareena took the cue and fluttered haltingly over to the top of the china cabinet.

"She's flying," I said. "Good for her!"

"She needs to be outside, though. She can't stay cooped up in here."

"Tell her that."

"I'm trying. Come on, girl. The window is just over that way. You keep going. That's it."

Netareena made a swoop of the dining room and fluttered back into the kitchen where she perched on the spigot in the sink. She bent her head and caught a drop of water in her beak.

"Smart bird," I said. "Now, if she could only figure out where the window is. How can she miss it? It's wide open. Try to coax her in that direction. I'm going to call Steph."

I dialed the number and received a recorded message in Italian. The voice sounded like Steph's, so I left a message in English, telling her we knew where the mattresses were and that we would move them to the cart. I apologized to her for the inconvenience and ended with "ciao."

Sue and I spent the next twenty minutes flapping our arms at Netareena as much as she was flapping her wings around the apartment. We chased her in and out of nearly every room before we finally gave up.

"She'll leave when she's ready to," I concluded.

"I hope she decides she's ready to leave by tomorrow because we're leaving the next day. Who's to say the house-keeper or the next batch of tenants will be as understanding as we've been?"

"Let's leave Netareena for the time being and attend to those mattresses," I suggested. "I feel bad that we didn't break up our rooftop hideaway this morning when we were cleaning the rest of the apartment. That way Steph would have found the mattresses in the closet where they belong."

"And we wouldn't have to be the ones hauling them down the stairs."

"Come on. How hard can it be? We'll figure out how to make a merit badge out of it. You would like that, wouldn't you?"

"Don't try to cheer me up," Sue said. "I'm too tired. And I'm still mad at the gondolier. I was looking forward to that gondola ride more than you can imagine."

"So we'll go tomorrow. Domani. We'll find a respectable, pudgy, middle-aged, gondolier, and we won't even ask if he sings."

Sue managed a half smile. "Okay. We'll go tomorrow.

It'll give us something to look forward to on our last night."

"And we'll make sure we have enough cash on us so we can go for the hour tour. I mean, if we're going to do this, we should do it right."

"I agree. You've heard my motto before, haven't you?"

"I'm not sure. Which motto?"

"'Buy the best and cry about it once.'"

My expression didn't change.

"Don't you get it?"

I shook my head.

"It means, if you're going to buy something worthwhile, go ahead and pay for the best. You may cry about having to spend so much up front, but that's better than buying something cheap or inadequate and then crying about it when it breaks or doesn't work. You end up having to go back and purchase the best one later just so you have one that works."

I still didn't fully see how her logic related to the hourlong gondola ride versus the half-hour ride. But I did understand more clearly why it had been so painful to Sue last year when she and Jack moved into a smaller house and had to cut way back on any upgrades. All the extra money had to go toward accommodating Jack's wheelchair. The front ramp, the walk-in shower, and the low kitchen and bathroom counters all had cost extra. Sue's artistic touches were limited to a new bedspread and a larger mirror over the bathroom sink. I filed away her comments and decided that the gondola ride was important to her because it was a final luxury on an already luxurious trip.

Sue checked on Netareena one more time, and then we headed up to the roof to dismantle our hideaway. We worked quickly in the gathering dark, pulling up the bedding first. Trying to remember the angle we had bent the mattresses when we brought them up to the roof, Sue and I figured out how to turn them to maneuver them down the stairs.

"You're right," Sue said after the first mattress made it through the narrow passageway. "It's a lot easier with gravity on our side."

With a concerted effort, we removed everything from the roof. Making sure the door with the ancient latch was closed securely, we shuffled the mattresses down the hall on their sides. Once we reached the front door, Sue and I each took one side of the first mattress and lugged it to the top of the wide, marble stairs. We only had to move it ten stairs down to a landing, then a turn, ten more stairs, a landing, a turn and ten more.

"Too bad we can't just drop it out the window," Sue said.

"This won't be hard," I said. "We probably could push it down, and it would slide on its own to the landing. Let's try it."

We placed the mattress flat at the top of the stairs and gave it a shove. It went down two stairs before stopping and teetering. I walked down, bent over, and pushed it the rest of the way.

"You look like a mattress cowboy," Sue said. "Should I get you a cattle prod?"

I maneuvered the mattress around on the landing and stopped at the top of the next level of stairs to catch my breath. An idea came to me.

"Sue, have you ever been mattress surfing?"

She looked down at me. "No."

"Me neither." Then, without stopping to allow even a glimmer of logic to speak up inside my head, I flung myself belly first on the positioned mattress and sailed down the ten marble stairs.

"Sweet peaches, Jenna! What are you doing?" Sue ran down the two flights of stairs and came to my side, looking ready to perform CPR.

I was laughing so hard I couldn't tell her that nothing was broken. "That was awesome!" I finally peeped out.

"For you, maybe. I thought I was going to have to try to call an ambulance. How do they get an ambulance down these canals?"

"I don't need an ambulance."

"Who says the ambulance was for you? You'd like to have given me a heart attack."

"Try it, Sue. It's so fun. You're well padded."

"Thanks a lot."

I laughed again at my grammatical blunder. "I meant

the mattress will protect you since the mattress is so well padded."

"No thank you."

"Fine. Then step back. I'm going again."

Before Sue could protest, I positioned the mattress at the top of the final flight of stairs and did an even more daring belly leap onto the cushioned sled. As had been the case the first time, the front of the mattress hit the wall, stopping me unscathed.

"I can't believe you're doing that."

I rolled over on my back and laughed merrily. The sound echoed up the stairwell. Covering my mouth, I lowered my voice. "I'll come up and get the next one."

Sue stood back, as I repeated my performance with the second mattress. For a girl who grew up in Minnesota with months' worth of snow and every sort of sled and toboggan available, I was primed for this indoor event.

"Come on, Sue." I felt rosy-cheeked as I looked up at her still-leery expression. "Didn't you ever sled as a kid?"

"No."

"Then think of it as busting a bronco. You just hold on for the ride."

"I never busted a bronco, either. Why do people always think that, if you're from Texas, you have experience with cattle?"

"I forgot. You were the city-girl debutant. Didn't you ever have a Slip 'N Slide in your backyard?"

"Yes."

"Well, then consider that your training for this mattress ride." I looked up at her with an impish grin. "Only two more flights of stairs. This is your last chance."

She hesitated, so I took off, still cracking myself up. As I positioned the mattress for the final batch of stairs, Sue sauntered down to the landing where I stood.

"What if we both went?" she asked timidly. It intrigued me that Sue could be fearless about things that daunted me like cooking for a group, yet she froze up in the presence of uncomplicated pleasures like this.

"Sure, we'll go next to each other. Hold on to the side, not the front. You want the mattress, not your head, to hit the wall first."

Fortunately the first mattress was currently lined up against the wall at the end of the stairs, so even if Sue's head did hit first, it would collide with the mattress and not the stucco.

Sue worked hard at having fun. She made sure she was in the right position, that her hands weren't too sweaty, and that she had a firm grip.

"Ready?"

She closed her eyes, gritted her teeth, and said, "Go!"

I pushed us off. We sailed even faster with the added weight. Our ride was over before Sue had a chance to squeal. Soft-landing against the other mattress, I laughed as hard as I had all the other times.

Sue opened her eyes wide and surveyed the successful landing. She didn't laugh on the outside, but it looked as if some childlike giggle box inside her had been shaken loose.

"Let's do it again!"

"That means we have to carry one of the mattresses back up the stairs."

"So? Isn't that what you do with a sled? Come on! I want to go down with my eyes open this time. I missed it."

We lugged the mattress back up the stairs and positioned it.

"This time," I said, "don't think so much. Just jump on and ride."

"By myself?"

"Yes. By yourself. I'm throwing you into the deep end. Remember?"

"Oh, yes, I'd almost forgotten that request. Okay. Tell me what to do again. I just jump on and then what?"

"That's it. Just get on and slide. It's not rocket science. Go on. Jump!"

Sue jumped. If she had been jumping into a pool, her maneuver would have been likened to a belly flop. But the important thing was that she jumped. The mattress did its part, and when she landed, her squeals of laughter could be heard throughout the building.

I heard one of the neighbor's doors open a few floors above us. Motioning with both my hands to keep the noise down I whispered, "We're waking the neighbors."

"I'll be quiet," she said. "I'm going again."

I chuckled softly, as Sue pulled the mattress up the stairwell by herself with red-faced determination.

"I'll be right back," I told her in a whisper.

"Where are you going?"

"I have to get the camera. This is too fun not to capture on film. Besides, I don't know about your kids, but Callie will never believe I did this. I need pictures to prove it."

Sue instinctively smoothed back her hair. I laughed. "Uh, let me put it this way: Don't bother."

"Do me a favor then, will you? When you come back with the camera, bring me a bandana or something to cover my head."

I did one better than just the requested bandana. I also returned with the colander we had used to strain the pasta.

"Protective gear!" The grin that accompanied my declaration was far too comical, and Sue knew it. She took my challenge and tied the colander down with her bandana. I laughed so hard and suppressed it so effectively that all the giggles came out in the form of tears. I couldn't see well enough to line up the picture.

"Here, let me." Sue grabbed the camera, held it at arm's length and snapped a photo of herself.

My sides ached from holding in my amusement. One thing I was learning about Sue was that, even though it was a challenge to get her to jump into the deep end, once she was there, she turned into a mermaid.

"All systems go." Sue took her position this time by sitting on the mattress and folding her arms in front of her, as if she were riding a magic carpet.

"Wait!" It was so hard to keep our voices low. "I'm going to go down a flight to catch a shot of you coming toward me."

"Whatever you do, stay out of my way," Sue said with an air of authority.

I scooted into position. "Spaghetti-Head, start your engines!"

Sue gave herself a push off and tried to keep her sultan-like position all the way down. I snapped pictures one right after the other as the mattress came toward me. On the second to the last step, Sue leaned to one side and the mattress compensated by coming right at me. Before I could move away, my body turned into the bobsled guardrail. I fell into the mattress. Sue and I tumbled like a couple of crash dummies.

"You were supposed to move!" Sue tried not to laugh.

"You were supposed to steer!" I countered.

"And both of you were supposed to answer your phone up in the apartment."

We turned to see Steph standing just inside the door that led to the entry garage space.

"You be Calvin, I'll be Hobbs," Sue said in my ear, comically indicating which one of us she thought should turn into the deaf and mute stuffed animal in this unreal scenario.

I swallowed back a huge urge to bust up and tried to face Steph with a sober expression.

"Are those by any chance the mattresses?" she asked.

I nodded, still not trusting myself to open my mouth due to all the laughter I was working so hard to swallow.

"And should I even ask what you're doing?"

I glanced sideways at Sue. She kept looking straight ahead, and in a serious tone she said, "I understand the Jamaicans have a bobsled team. We thought we would help to develop a land version of the sport for the Venetians."

I couldn't believe Sue came up with that. The ball of chuckles tangled up in my throat bounced up to the roof of my mouth. I didn't know what would happen if I let them out, so I kept quiet and tried to regain my composure.

Sue was uncannily composed. She untied her helmet and held it out to Steph, silently inviting her to come play with us. We were all out of our best jokes. If Steph was going to call us on the carpet for what we were doing, or should I say call us on the marble, this was her chance.

She paused only a moment before a wide grin took over her countenance. "You two totally rock my world! I'm in. Where do I get on?"

Twenty

hen the morning light slid through the cracks in the shutters of the princess suite, it took me a moment to remember where I was.

"Ohh," Sue groaned. "What time is it?"

"I don't know. Where's my watch?"

"Where's my head?" Sue groaned again. "I ache all over."

I felt around on the nightstand for my watch and squinted to read the dial. "It's ten after eight." I sat up and stretched. "We should get going if we want to beat the tourist rush to San Marco Square."

"How can it be after eight already?" Sue rolled over with great effort. "I think I have a hangover."

"A mattress-sledding hangover?"

"I think it wasn't the sledding so much as laughing so

hard. Is it possible to release too many endorphins and put your liver into overdrive?"

"I don't think so. The laughing was good for us. I think maybe the going out with Steph afterwards for triple scoops of gelato was what could have put the strain on your liver."

"It was good, though, wasn't it? What was that one flavor you had? Not the chocolate."

"Grapefruit." I rose and pulled up the sheets over my bed in a fluffy fashion.

"That was it. Grapefruit and chocolate. That was so good. An unlikely combination, but definitely the best gelato combination so far."

"How's Netareena?" I asked. "Is she still in her box?"

When we finally had returned to the apartment late the night before, we found Netareena had returned to her box nest in the kitchen corner. Both of us were surprised she hadn't yet flown the coop now that she was able to flap her way around the apartment. Sue had brought the box into our bedroom and positioned her on the floor beside the nightstand.

Leaning over the side of her bed, Sue reported. "She's gone. Watch where you step. She could be hopping around on the floor."

I looked up instead of down. I figured it was more likely Netareena would be perched on top of the buxom green dresser or one of the ornately framed mirrors than hopping on the floor.

"I don't see her," I said. "I'm going to open the shutters."

"No!" Sue rolled over, her back to the windows. "Make the brightness go away."

"You really aren't a morning person," I said, stating the obvious. I pulled open the tall wooden doors. The adjustable slats in these wooden, true "Venetian blinds" rattled. The golden brightness of the new day engulfed me.

"Awk," Sue groaned. "I'm melting… melting…"

I ignored her complaints and stepped out on the balcony, breathing in deeply. The fragrance of the sullen canal below rose to greet me with a thick, moldy, fishy scent. The air was still. No breeze existed on this side of the palace like the one we had experienced on the roof or during our afternoon nap on the sitting room couches our first day.

"Phew! I think it's better on this side later in the day." Closing the shuttered doors and going back inside, I was greeted by words of appreciation for "turning off the light."

"I'm going to make some coffee and take a shower," I said.

"Good. I'm going back to sleep."

I could never fall asleep once I was awake in the morning. Sue seemed to have no problem doing just that.

My bathing procedure started with the trickling

shower in the bathroom and was followed by my moving everything to the kitchen sink. I planned to wash my hair the way Sue had a few days earlier, sticking my head in the marble sink and making use of the water pressure.

Netareena was waiting for me in the kitchen. She was perched on the edge of the kitchen sink but flew away as I approached with my towel and shampoo.

"Don't be frightened. It's just me. I'm going to wash my hair. You can have your watering hole back in a moment." I stuck my head under the warm running water and lathered up. I could hear Netareena chirping at me from some corner of the kitchen. It felt like I was in an organic shampoo commercial where the birds chirp while the woman luxuriates in her shampoo's herbal fragrances.

I tipped my head under the running water, ready to rinse all the shampoo down the drain when suddenly the water stopped. I waited. I tapped the spigot. I kicked at the pipe under the sink and dripped soapsuds everywhere. My hair was only partially rinsed. All the lathered-up suds were racing down my forehead as well as popping in my ears.

"Come on, water! Start again, will you?"

I waited another minute before reaching for one of the plastic bottles of drinking water. Opening it with my wet fingers, I proceeded to pour the cold water over my head. Now that was a brutal wake-up call. The suds remained, so two more bottles were required to complete the rinse cycle.

Shivering, I wrapped the towel around my numb skull and saw Netareena flying around the room. No doubt she was checking out where all the muffled yet primal wails were coming from.

Coffee was next on the list. I filled the coffeepot with bottled water. This was my first time figuring out all the kitchen gizmos by myself. I didn't have the knack Sue did to adjust the flame just right so that the water would percolate up through the metal tube in the middle of the coffeepot and bubble up like a fountain over the container of coffee grounds. My flame must have been too high, or else I put in too much water.

The steaming, gurgling mess oozed over the rim of the old metal coffee percolator and doused its life-giving flame just as Sue came padding into the kitchen.

"What's going on?" she moaned, still squinting.

"The water is off again," I said. "And I think I just extinguished the pilot light on the stove."

"I heard all the banging, and then I smelled burned coffee."

"Sorry about that. I'm a mess in the kitchen without you, Sue. Now you know the truth."

She smiled, her eyes still half-closed. "Then I guess you weren't kidding when you asked me to come with you."

"You mean not kidding about needing you to help me cook for the men? No, I definitely wasn't exaggerating about that." I turned off all the knobs on the stove top and removed the messed-up coffeepot. "I'm also not exaggerating when I say I think we should get out of here before I manage to blow up something. Paolo will have to make our morning cappuccinos for us."

"You won't hear any arguments from me there. Let me just take a quick shower and…wait. There's no water, right?"

Sue managed what she called a washcloth bath with two bottles of water and a fresh-scented bottle of liquid shower wash. She wrestled amicably with her mass of unwashed curls and threatened to cut them all off. I'd heard those threats many times before, but so far the long hair remained.

She was ready to leave before I was because I'd gone looking for Netareena. The perky bird had escaped from the kitchen like a wise soul the minute she saw me with the box of matches trying to light the burner. And that was before the coffee bubbled over.

In my search for our flighty friend, I meandered through the dining room and into the open sitting room. I dearly missed the deep voices, the prayers, and Malachi's reading of the Psalms. The ceilings in these rooms may have been painted with pastel clouds and cherubs and the walls covered with frescos and tapestries, but in my mind's eye I saw them invisibly washed with the Word of God that lives and abides forever. His Word alone is eternal. That was a curious thought in this place of antiquity. There is old, and then there is eternal. I felt hungry for the eternal.

Sue felt hungry for good coffee. Or so she told me when she found me alone in the sitting room, deep in my morning meditations.

"I was looking for Netareena," I said.

"I have her."

"You do? Where?"

Sue held up one of the cloth shopping bags we had bought the first day at the grocery store.

"You didn't put her in the bag, did you? Say you didn't."

"Don't worry. It's not like I'm going to try to get her to produce eggs for me so I can sell them on the street. She was on the kitchen counter, and the bag was the best way to scoop her up."

"So what are you going to do with her?"

"I don't know. I was thinking of taking her with us."

"Back to Dallas?"

"No, to San Marco Square. I thought I'd let her go there with all the other birds so she wouldn't feel alone."

We stood in the sitting room and argued. It would have been a much friendlier argument if we had at least sat in the sitting room and discussed the options calmly.

With each reason I presented on the side of leaving Netareena as she was, alone in the apartment, Sue became more passionate about taking the timid bird out of there.

"She needs to get out of these familiar surroundings,"

Sue said. "She has to go be with other birds so she can remember who she was before she had a major setback."

I gave up. It didn't matter, really. Sue was talking about Netareena as if she were a person and not a little fallen sparrow. I knew our argument would matter even less after we had some coffee and one of Lucia's breakfast rolls.

Thus began our final full day as guests of Mama Venezia. With Sue's "bird in the hand," or should I say, "bird in the bag," we made our sweetly familiar trek to Lucia's.

She was surprised to see us. I think because we walked through her door nearly three hours later than our usual visit. Most of her morning offerings already had been snatched up. However, two fresh baci were waiting for Sue and me. Lucia presented them to us with a glimmer in her amber-flecked eyes.

The night before, while Steph had joined us for after-tobogganing gelato, I had asked her to write a note to Lucia in Italian for me. The sentiment was a simple thank-you for her kindness, along with my address, "Just in case you ever come to Dallas and want to stay with someone who speaks about six words of Italian."

Steph thought the note was "gracious" and "sweet." Although she didn't know Lucia and had never been to that panetteria, she was sure Lucia would appreciate the gesture.

Steph was right. When Lucia read the note, she got

teary-eyed and came around the counter to give Sue and me big Italian mama hugs. Both of us wore a dusting of pastry flour on the front of us the rest of the day.

Paolo wasn't quite as mushy when we showed up at one of his outdoor tables and ordered cappuccinos like pros. He flirted with us and brought us extra sugar cubes. At least we think his string of Italian was flirting. He could have been chewing us out for bringing our own breakfast rolls.

We had gone for the same table where we had sat almost a week ago on that first Sunday morning in Venice. We even sat in our same chairs. The same violinist was standing in the same pocket of shade and playing the same Vivaldi tune.

"He's gotten even better," Sue said as she sipped her cappuccino.

"I'm not surprised, if he's been playing it every day."

Sue looked across at him with a look of admiration. "I don't think he's been playing that piece every day. I think he's been honoring that piece of music every day. He embraces it; he loves it. That's why he's gotten better."

I would have brushed off Sue's philosophizing that morning, but her own words made her cry. Her tears were silent and ceaseless. Those are the deepest kind. I know because I had cried tears like that over my frozen milk when we ordered our first breakfast gelato here. My tears were incited by something simple—the look. That kind and encompassing way that Sue looks at me to let me know she accepts me just the way I am.

I felt much more whole this morning than I had that morning. So much had happened in such a short time.

I longed to know what was causing Sue's tears now. What had changed in her this week? What was it about the Vivaldi music that got to her the way it did?

"What piece is that he's playing?" I asked.

Sue spoke through her tears. "*Four Seasons*. He's playing 'Spring' right now."

"A time of new beginnings," I said more to myself than to Sue.

She nodded and added, "A season of refreshment." The tears kept coming; she didn't try to stop them.

One of the parts of our ebb and flow that had worked so well during the week was that Sue and I let each other just "be." I'd made an effort to stop being bossy and to honor what she had asked earlier. I didn't "diagnose" her, and I had put aside my great ambition to fix her. But seeing her pouring out so much now in deep tears, I didn't feel that I could stand back and just let her be. I needed to coax the truth out of her heart.

"Sue, what is it?"

"The music. The bird. God sending goodness and mercy out to follow me. All of it."

I didn't understand. Why would any of those things make her cry?

She reached into her bag and pulled out her notebook where she had been listing the gelato ratings. "Read this." She opened to a page where she had written a single verse.

"Repent therefore and be converted, that your sins may be blotted out, so that times of refreshing may come from the presence of the Lord."

The first part seemed rather harsh. I wasn't sure why Sue would have written down a verse about repenting and sins being blotted out. I looked at her for an explanation.

"That verse was on Malachi's list," she said. "It was one of the passages he read yesterday morning. I saw the reference when you showed me the list that fell out of his Bible."

"You glanced at the list one time and remembered that reference?" I knew I shouldn't be surprised. To Sue, it must have been a piece of the puzzle to help decode her life map.

"I looked it up last night," she said.

"When?"

"After midnight. I couldn't sleep. I'm glad you didn't hear me get up. I went into the sitting room and took your Bible and my flashlight and notebook. I hope you don't mind."

"Of course not." I smiled to myself. Every worthwhile woman's retreat I'd ever attended listed on the brochure that we were to bring our Bible, notebook, pen, and flashlight. I always thought it odd to list those along with sunscreen, bath towel, and spending money. As if we weren't old enough or responsible enough to think to bring those things.

Listening to Sue, I knew why women needed to have those tools at hand whenever they went on a retreat. In the same way that I'd written down the message "You're not done yet" so many months ago, Sue had written down this verse.

I felt as if I were just beginning to see what it meant for me not to be done yet. I was ready for what was to come next. After all that had happened this week, I could see I had entered a new season. A springtime of beginnings.

Now Sue was seeing something clearly. Something about this verse had sliced into her heart like a two-edged sword during her midnight encounter with the Spirit of God.

Understanding now the source of her stream of tears, I leaned forward. "Tell me, Sue. I want to hear. What is it?"

Her words came out low and lean. "I need to turn back to God. I need to trust Him the way I did before Jack's accident."

I nodded. I knew such trust was a process that involved a lot of forgiveness. I'd gone down those steps before. I'd gone through years of processing. I probably could have "tobogganed" down those steps a lot faster if I had been willing to jump into the process of forgiveness as easily as I'd jumped on the mattress last night. But for the most part, I took one step at a time, carrying all the weight of my anger and disappointment with me.

Sue, it seemed, was ready to jump. She had solved the biggest piece of the puzzle. Turning back to God all the way, trusting Him no matter what. I understood those steps better than Sue realized.

"I've seen it this week in your life, Jenna. It doesn't matter what goes wrong with the plan for life, does it? We still can start over. We can go back to God anytime."

I nodded, even though she didn't need my affirmation. She had grasped onto truth and wasn't about to let go.

"It's all so obvious to me now. God is great at visual aids, isn't He?"

I wasn't sure what she meant.

Sue gave a little sniff and turned her eyes toward the violin player. "Four seasons? Spring? Beginnings? It's like God knew that if I didn't catch what He was trying to tell me in the verse, then He knew I'd hear it in the music. He's inviting me to enter a new season. A season of refreshing."

I smiled as the high violin notes rose on the morning breeze and came washing over us.

"But first," Sue said, the tears beginning to flow once more, "I have to turn back to God. All the way."

I reached over and gave her hand a squeeze, conveying the deep-hearted understanding I had for her and for what she was saying.

"Go ahead, Sis. Jump into the deep end."

Twenty-One

I'm not sure Paolo knew what to do with the two crying, praying, laughing women who occupied the corner table that morning. He brought us a second round of cappuccinos at no charge and left a stack of square cocktail napkins for us to sop up our tears.

The violinist kept playing, as if mysteriously motivated by our emotions. Sue explained to me why she thought of the musician as honoring the music, embracing it, and loving it. She told me that echoed what she wanted to do when she returned home to her husband.

"I want to honor him, embrace him, and love him—and get better at it every day," she said.

With awkward words I told Sue that I believed it could be well with our souls even when it might never be well with our circumstances.

She nodded, and that's when I knew that, for both of us, a season of refreshing definitely had come. And it came, as Sue's verse said, from being in the Lord's presence.

By the time we had pulled ourselves together and were ready to take our swishy, sightseeing skirts to San Marco Square, the morning was almost passed. Sue had been checking periodically on Netareena in her protected sack and periodically fed the bird crumbs from her baci, making sure the bag stayed in the shade.

"It's time to let her go," Sue said, as we rose from the café table, leaving behind a pile of used cocktail napkins.

"Do you still want to take her to San Marco Square?"

Sue paused. Her argument earlier that morning had been that Netareena needed to be around other birds. She needed to get out of her familiar surroundings and remember who she had been before the trauma hit her. I hadn't understood at the time, but now I could see that Sue was projecting her own experience on this little wounded bird.

I think Sue saw it, too. Whether her initial aspirations for Netareena had been subconscious or deliberate, Sue now seemed to have a different view of what needed to be done for her small charge.

Bending down and opening the mouth of the shopping bag, Sue gently shook it. "Come on. It's okay. You can come out now. This is a good place to start over."

Netareena emerged from the sack with a string of little

hops. She paused in the brightness of the full sun for only a moment before flapping her wings and taking off.

"Fly! Be free!" I called out as she flew to the top of the lone tree in the middle of Campo Apostoli.

"Now I'm really ready," Sue said. "Really, really ready for anything."

We hiked across footbridges and down narrow alleyways, caught up in a crush of sightseers all the way to the Piazza San Marco. Even so, our first impression, as we stepped into what Napoleon had dubbed "the most beautiful living room in Europe," was how stunning the square was. The arched-front buildings on either side lined the huge plaza in perfect symmetry.

Sue and I stopped to take it all in. I wasted no time in pulling out the camera and attempting to capture the magnificence. Ahead of us was the rocket ship bell tower that Sam said had once been a lighthouse guarding the opening of the Grand Canal. Directly behind us was the clock tower. A huge white statue of a winged lion with his paw on an open book stood on a wide ledge atop the fourth floor. Above the lion on the clock tower's roof was a gigantic bell. Two grand statues of bronze men stood on either side of the bell. Both of them held long-handled anvils poised to strike the bell on the hour.

To our right stretched the long, open piazza. Two outdoor cafés looked like they were doing a brisk business. The one on the right had yellow chairs at the small tables.

The other café, across from us on the left side of the piazza, had tan, wicker-backed chairs.

Being in such proximity, I guessed the competition between the two rivals had continued for many years. Each had its own "colors" and distinct clientele.

"That café on the left," Sue told me, as she consulted her tour book, "is the Caffe Florian. Hemmingway used to go there. So did Mark Twain, Charles Dickens, Lord Byron, Henry James and—"

As soon as I stopped recognizing the names of the famous people on Sue's list, I interrupted her. "Would you mind if we just have a look around and do some of our own discovering?"

She didn't mind my suggestion. The tour book went back in her bag, and we spent the next four and a half hours being swept along into the nucleus of Venezia with thousands of other tourists. We saw it all. The view from the top of the crowded, claustrophobia-inducing bell tower, the tour of San Marco Basilica's interior, and a short-ened, self-guided tour of the Doge's palace.

My general impression of it all was, "so much." There was so much gold. So much art. So much detail in the mosaic tiles, and so much history. We were surrounded by people, by many languages, by more odors and sounds than I could take in.

I was on overload—sensory, emotional, and mental overload.

Sue took it all in. When we returned to Dallas and started to tell our stories, Sue remembered everything about the hours we spent at San Marco Square. I think her heart and mind were so wide open that she had all kinds of space to take in every drop of the experience. I was open but already full of the stuff that had made the trip most memorable to me.

The parts of that day that I do remember are the simple moments. One of them happened inside the basilica. When we first entered, everything in the cross-shaped church appeared dark since it had been so bright outside. Slowly, as our eyes adjusted and the filtered light changed, we saw the details in the tiled mosaics. The atmosphere was different from any church I'd ever been in. It felt mystical. The Eastern-Byzantine influence was like nothing I'd seen in other European churches.

Inside the huge dome was a breathtaking tile mosaic that filled the dome in separate frames, like a movie. The pictures told the story of Adam and Eve in the Garden of Eden. In one of the arches next to the dome was another picture story. This one was of Noah and the Great Flood. The frames were all worked in bright-colored tiles that could have come from Murano.

Two features of that mural captured my attention. One was the image of Noah letting the dove out to see if the land was dry. The releasing of small birds was memorable for obvious reasons.

I pointed it out to Sue, and she nodded and smiled.

The other detail in the portrayal that caught our attention was that the first two animals in line to board Noah's ark were none other than lions. Lions, lions everywhere.

The actual burial place of St. Mark was difficult to see due to the swarms of visitors crowded around guides explaining in several languages what the tourists were viewing. A marble canopy with carved columns and an incredible altarpiece in thick gold detailed intricate scenes from the New Testament. That part of the tour was just too much for me. I quietly shuffled out and found an open pew where I could sit and reflect.

Sue wasn't ready to stop until I convinced her we should find some much needed food. We hadn't eaten anything since our morning baci.

"I don't want to miss anything," she said.

To solve that problem, we sat at one of the outdoor tables at the Florian Café so we could watch all the action around the piazza. The big attraction was the unceasing feeding of the pigeons.

Vendors at carts sold small bags of corn for one euro. People of all sizes, shapes, colors, and ages poured the corn into their hands and held them out for the tame pigeons, which perched on the open palms and pecked away as if the birds hadn't seen food for a month.

"You would think those birds would be overfed," Sue commented, as we finished our ham and cheese *pannini*.

"They keep coming out of nowhere." I watched a little boy timidly hold out his handful of corn. He quickly pulled away when the first bird tried to peck a kernel.

"Are you going to make fun of me if I buy some corn to feed the pigeons?" Sue asked.

"No, of course not. I'm going to take your picture!"

After we paid for our late lunch, we strolled across the plaza to where it seemed less congested. Sue bought a bag of corn, and I readied the camera. She sedately poured five or six kernels in her hand and held it out, waiting for a taker. No pigeons came her way.

Two teen boys were standing nearby. In broken English one of them said, "You want birds to come?"

"Yes, do y'all have a secret to get them to come?"

The boys exchanged glances that we should have interpreted as far too mischievous. But Sue was intent on attracting the birds, and I was concentrating on being ready to snap pictures. Neither Sue nor I saw what happened next.

All we knew was that, in one motion, both the boys dashed over to Sue and poured their corn packets over her head. Instantly three pigeons landed on her head and picnicked in her tussled cornfield.

I thought she would shake the birds and seed off her head as quickly as she could. But, to my surprise, she stood there, looking shocked yet saying, "Did you take a picture? Did you take a picture?"

I laughed as I slowly circled her, catching every angle of the birds in her red tree house.

"Jack is never going to believe this," I said.

"Hey, I'm not believing this," Sue said with a squeal.

"Sue, if you're thinking of asking me if your hair looks good in these shots, you can guess my answer."

"I wasn't going to ask," Sue said. "I'm not that much of a birdbrain."

She laughed so hard at her own joke that the birds flew away. Bending over and giving her hair a good shake and ruffling her scalp, she said, "Your turn. Hand over the camera, and I'll take some pictures of you."

I went with the more sedate pose of holding out my palms and had no trouble attracting the rousted pigeons, which came back for the last of the corn. Their beaks tickled as they went for the kernels in my hands. Their smooth gray feathers caught the late afternoon sun pouring over the piazza and reflected a dozen jewel-toned colors. I admired the up close view of the birds as much as all the inlaid gold-, ruby-, and sapphire-adorned works of art we had viewed in the man-made places of worship. God does a much better job of making works of art that reflect His glory.

The feeding of the pigeons was delightful and turned out to be a great ending to our long afternoon in the open-air "living room." It was one of those touristy things that, as you watch others, you think you don't want to do. But once we entered into the experience, it turned out to be a favorite memory.

To cap off our full and fabulous day, Sue and I went in pursuit of what turned out to be her favorite tourist custom. Sunset was approaching. We needed to find a gondola that came with just the right gondolier.

We found him along the waterfront near one of the great columns that rose into the night sky at the water's edge and guarded the entrance to the Piazza San Marco. A winged lion stood atop the column.

Our gondolier was sitting on a bench with several other gondoliers in front of the lined-up, waiting gondolas. His name was Matteo, and he was the only one of the lot who looked like he was over forty. He was also the only one who didn't look up at us and grin as we approached. That's why we chose Matteo. It was a good choice.

He spoke English and understood clearly when we said we wanted to see all we could in an hour's ride. We told him we didn't want to go down the Grand Canal like everyone else. We wanted to see his favorite parts of Venezia.

With a respectful nod, Matteo helped us into the padded seats of his carefully detailed gondola and backed up from the dock. Across from us, beyond a span of seawater, was the island of San Giorgio Maggiore, where the men had visited the Benedictine monks. From where Sue and I sat in the gondola, we had a perfect view of the lowering sun as it tossed a wide, loose knit shawl of golden light across the waters. A shawl to cover dear Venezia.

Matteo steered the gondola down what looked like a main canal opening. He leisurely pointed out the sights: the home where Marco Polo was born; the balcony on the home of Casanova; the oldest church in Venice; his personal favorite seafood restaurant.

"Their specialty is *seppia al nero*. It's very good."

"And what exactly is that?" Sue asked.

"Squid cooked in its own ink."

Sue made a face, and I knew we wouldn't seek out that restaurant for a late-night snack.

Taking the camera from me, Sue snapped a shot of the restaurant. Then she took a few close-up shots of me. She started to get into the fun of taking pictures and caught several of Matteo, with his steady posture, as he watched the canal ahead of us. This was a man who took his work seriously. We liked Matteo.

"Was your grandfather a gondolier?" Sue asked.

"Yes. And his grandfather and so on."

"That's so amazing to me. When did y'all start working as a gondolier?" Sue asked.

"I was seven." He went on to describe the intense training that included becoming fluent in other languages. Matteo spoke seven languages and had been doing this since he was fifteen.

My respect for the gondoliers rose as we listened to

Matteo. What he did was a dying art. During the winter months, he could go several weeks without picking up a single fare. I don't know if he told us all this to pique our sympathies so that we tipped him well at the end of the ride, but it worked. We parted with our money willingly. A significant reason for that was the final point of interest he showed us on our circular route back to the dock.

"Ahead of us you will see *Il Ponte dei Sospiri*. The Bridge of Sighs."

"I read about that," Sue said.

I gave her a little tap on the leg, motioning that we should let Matteo tell us his version. Sue snapped pictures of the covered passageway that was suspended two stories above the canal. The gray edifice was ornately decorated. Two windows were positioned like two eyes that had their lids closed. This was because the windows were covered on the inside with what looked like a permanent shade that had only enough slits to let in air.

"The prison is on this side. The court in the palace of the Doge is on the other side. When a prisoner was found guilty in the court, he would be taken across this bridge on his way to prison. Here he would take his last look at beautiful Venezia and sigh." Matteo demonstrated with a deep sigh. "This is why it is called The Bridge of Sighs."

As our gondola slowly passed under the structure, we looked at its underbelly. Sue drew in a deep breath and let out a long sigh.

I said, "Are you trying to see what the prisoners felt like?"

She shook her head and smiled softly. "I already know what a prison feels like. I'm sighing to see what if feels like to come out of prison and float away, a free woman."

For the rest of her life, I knew this place, this day, this bridge would be Sue's bridge of sighs. She was free.

And so was I.

So how do two free birds that are ready for the next season of life celebrate on such an evening? After Matteo helped us out of the gondola, we flitted right over to the nearest gelato bar, ordered big, and said ciao to Mama Venezia.

Epilogue

When, over the years, my mind wanders back to our trip to Venezia, I still think of her as a woman. In a strange way, I want to grow old the way she did.

Venezia candidly revealed her many sides to Sue and me that short week without once trying to hide her age. We watched her rise to her full height in the noonday sun and smile broadly on us, revealing rows of cracked and yellowing teeth. She blew baci at us from her curved footbridges painted a sweet shade of sienna. At sunset, her most dramatic hour, the Grand Dame stood still and let the sea-soaring birds adorn her faded tresses. On our final night there, Sue and I watched from a gondola as Venezia calmed her indigo waters and, with a sigh, invited strangers to come dance beneath her rising moon.

Venezia always will be a personality to me and not just another European city.

I miss Paolo and his corner café. I miss Lucia with her amber eyes and the way she presented us such gracious offerings of her daily bread. I miss the sound of Malachi's rumbling voice. I miss our view of the moon and stars from the rooftop.

Both Sue and I miss the water that surrounded us every day and lazily floated under all the footbridges we crossed. We miss the way the morning light changed the deep night waters into white wine colors. We miss the palace and the simple kitchen that had no oven.

And yes, of course, we miss the gelato. We've tried imposters in the U.S. that have advertised themselves as "Italian gelato," but sadly they are all frauds. We know gelato. As a matter of fact, some might consider us to be experts when it comes to Venetian gelato. At least we're certain we could earn a merit badge in that field.

Since that exceptional adventure, when Sue and I found ourselves "victims of grace," we have watched our small lives expand. Goodness and mercy have remained hot on our trail. And our trail, believe it or not, has led us to nine countries.

In some ways, my life went from being an "offering," like Malachi's eggs, and turned into a commitment. I was the chicken. In more ways than one. Sue and I now go to visit women who serve in full-time ministry. We go because sometimes they need an older sister to come along and help to brush the shame off them, for whatever reason.

There isn't a real science to it. We pray together about each invitation. We wait for the money for the trip to arrive, and it always comes in unexpected ways. Then we pack. I pack an easy-to-understand Bible translation, a new notebook, a pen, and a flashlight. Those items aren't for me, but for the woman I'm going to visit.

Sue packs what she calls her "Sisterchicks Survival Kit." Each kit is different, depending on what Sue finds to tuck inside, but all of them have something yummy to eat, something sweet to smell, and something uplifting to read. Once we took new underwear because the woman had let us know that was her greatest need. That time the gift was truly "uplifting" for her.

The first country we flew to was Ukraine. Goodness and mercy had to be following us through customs when we arrived because the airport inspector wanted to know why we were "smuggling" in so many bags of chocolate chips.

"Cookies," I told him, even though I wanted to nod at Sue and say it was her idea. "I've come to bake cookies for my friend in Kiev."

"You have come all this way to bake cookies?" he asked.

I nodded. Then I showed him the recipe on the back of the bag. He confiscated one of the bags for "inspection."

Deborah cried pretty much the whole first day we were there. Sergei hadn't told her we were coming so the poor thing was in shock. Our first batch of cookies brought her around, and she stopped crying long enough to eat them while they were still warm. We had to coax her into the luxurious bubble bath we prepared on our second day, complete with vanilla-scented candles to sweeten the least lovely room in their small apartment. After that we made Deborah take a nap while Sue fixed way too much pasta, and I mopped the floors and did the laundry.

By the third day, Deborah was ready to go out laughing, and boy, did we! When we left, Deborah had a clean house, a freshened heart, and a new smile. Sergei actually cried when he dropped us off at the airport. He said we had given him back his wife.

After that the invitations started coming from places Sue and I had never heard of. One time, the answer to our prayers about whether to travel to a certain destination was clearly, No, don't go this time. We still don't know why. But all the other times the money has arrived shortly after the invitation, and off we would go.

The most unique way the funds have arrived so far was when I walked into an appliance store and an alarm system went off. It turned out I was customer number ten thousand, and the prize was a double-wide refrigerator. How's that for just showing up? I didn't need a new refrigerator so I sold it to a friend at work, and that's how we financed our fifth Sisterchicks Hospitality Trip. That one was to Indonesia.

By that trip, Sue and I had a fairly good idea of what to take and what to do once we arrived. We listen to the women and tease them like we're already close friends. We read to their children and watch over their little flock so the women can steal a few hours of solitude or with their husbands. We laugh aloud. A lot.

I love it when they let me wrap my motherly arms around them and pray for them. I whisper in their ear, "Grace on you," and they always cry.

Sue and I make sure we read psalms to them every morning. On our last night, we take them aside with a pan of water and a towel. We kneel down and wash their feet. With a wonderful sigh, we tell these warrior women that what they are doing in serving the Lord has not gone unnoticed.

Then we cry happy tears all the way home.

Sue likes to tell people that we're couriers. We cross all kinds of borders to smuggle in goodness and mercy. And usually some form of chocolate.

My sister-in-law is a different woman from the nail-biting person who went to Venezia with me. Sue is a free woman. Jack is so proud of her. I am, too. Even when I watched her drawl all over herself in nine different countries.

I am a free woman as well. My past didn't disqualify me for this. If anything, after all the stories I've listened to, I would say my experiences prepared me for what I do.

And what exactly do I do? It's so simple that I almost missed it. I go where Jesus asks me to go and I feed His lambs.

Discussion Guide

1. Jenna felt as if God was telling her "You're not done yet." Have you ever felt the same thing? If so, what happened next in your life?

2. A new season had begun for Sue and Jenna. The burdened Sisterchicks at the beginning of the book became "victims of grace" in Venice and were ready to take flight again. When has God touched you in such a remarkable way that you could also claim to be a "victim of grace"?

3. Sue and Jenna had both weathered demolishing storms in their lives. Jenna's recipe for healing any sort of broken heart starts with equal parts truth and acceptance, then add the patient understanding of a true friend. Have you had a friend share this "recipe" with you during a troubling time in your life? How did it affect you?

4. When her husband left, Jenna found out that God didn't answer her prayers the way she wanted Him to. Even though she didn't recognize it at the time, the grace of His presence was sufficient. If you've ever been frustrated over unanswered prayer, how did you come to terms with this?

5. Jenna encouraged Sue to dive into the deep end of life so she could experience the refreshment that comes from taking that plunge. In what ways have you dived out of your comfort zones? What were the results?

6. On the boat when Marco winked at Jenna, it dug up her buried loneliness, her longing to be married to a man who would love her forever and never leave her. Share a time when you've had to conquer dragons of doubt and vultures of self-pity. What helped you through this troubling time?

7. When Sue gave Jenna "the smile," Jenna knew they were truly sisters. We are blessed to find Sisterchicks in many shapes—whether by blood or circumstances. Share about one of your Sisterchicks and how that relationship continues to grow.

8. Jenna told Sue, "Shame off you." Discuss the circumstances that led Jenna to say this to her sisterchick. Have you ever felt like Sue? When we open up and share with others the deepest struggles of our hearts, healing can begin, which leads us to say, "Shame off me!" And once we've done that, God's amazing grace shows up to fill us with hope and peace. If you are able, share your deepest aches with the group. And as each person shares, respond to them by saying "grace on you."

9. "Slice, chew, and swallow slowly" the peace that comes from immersing yourself in God's Word. Share your favorite Psalms and why it has become your air, food, and water to sustain you.

10. Jenna was told that showing love to a stranger is the definition of hospitality. In what ways have you reached out to the world around you and shown them God's love? How does that act of hospitality feel different from showing love to your friends or family?

11. After Jenna told Sam and Sergei the story of her marriage and divorce, their acceptance, understanding, and lack of judgment filled Jenna with a feeling of grace, freeing her from shame. Can you relate to Jenna's experience in any way? If so, how?

12. Jenna's internal response to Sam and Sergei's encouragement to "Feed His sheep" was to doubt that she had anything to offer. Often we spend so much time thinking about what we can't do, that we miss what we can do through the ways we are uniquely gifted. Share one way in which you're gifted and how that has been developed over the years.

13. Sam told Jenna, "I'm beginning to think that 90 percent of what we should be doing as believers is to just show up." Can you think of a time in your life when you just showed up and God's Spirit took it from there?

14. Showing up is a lot easier when the baggage of the past is left behind. Travel light! What is the baggage you need to let go of today?

More SISTERCHICK® Adventures by
ROBIN JONES GUNN

SISTERCHICKS ON THE LOOSE!

Zany antics abound when best friends Sharon and Penny take off on a midlife adventure to Finland, returning home with a new view of God and a new zest for life.

SISTERCHICKS DO THE HULA!

It'll take more than an unexpected stowaway to keep two middle-aged sisterchicks from reliving their college years with a little Waikiki wackiness—and learning to hula for the first time.

SISTERCHICKS IN SOMBREROS!

Two Canadian sisters embark on a journey to claim their inheritance—beachfront property in Mexico—not expecting so many bizarre, wacky problems! But there's nothing a little coconut cake can't cure...

SISTERCHICKS DOWN UNDER!

Kathleen meets Jill at the Chocolate Fish café in New Zealand, and they instantly forge a friendship. Together they fall head over heels into a deeper sense of God's love.

SISTERCHICKS SAY OOH LA LA!

Painting toenails and making promises under the canopy of a princess bed seals a friendship for life! Fifty years of ups and downs find Lisa and Amy still Best Friends Forever...and off on an unforgettable Paris rendezvous!

www.sisterchicks.com

Can't get enough of ROBIN JONES GUNN!

Christy Miller COLLECTION

Robin's beloved *Christy Miller* series is now available for the first time in collectible 3-in-1 hardback editions for the teen girls in your life.

Christy Miller Collection, Volume 1
Book 1: *Summer Promise*, Book 2: *A Whisper and a Wish*, Book 3: *Yours Forever*

Christy Miller Collection, Volume 2
Book 4: *Surprise Endings*, Book 5: *Island Dreamer*, Book 6: *A Heart Full of Hope*

Christy Miller Collection, Volume 3
Book 7: *True Friends*, Book 8: *Starry Night*, Book 9: *Seventeen Wishes*

Christy Miller Collection, Volume 4
Available June 2006!
Book 10: *A Time to Cherish*, Book 11: *Sweet Dreams*, Book 12: *A Promise Is Forever*

www.ChristyMillerAndFriends.com

Sisterchicks Down Under!

Age is just a number, right?

That's what I thought until three years ago when my younger brother opened his big mouth. He was on his way to Mexico to settle the legal details on some property his wife had inherited when he stopped by our home in Southern California. His life seemed brimming with new adventures, while Tony and I were riding the overly-committed-to-the-schedule freight train we had been on since we got married.

Over dinner my brother joked about his receding hairline. "You know, Kathleen, you're halfway there yourself."

"No I'm not." I pulled at the strands of my straight brown hair to prove that my dependable mane wasn't falling out.

"I meant your age. You turned forty-five last month, right? You could be halfway done." He seemed to wait for me to do the math.

I always hated math.

I felt as if an equation had etched itself on the chalkboard of my mind: $45 + x = ?$

I didn't know the answer.

What had my forty-five years added up to so far? What was the value of x that would fill the remaining years? What would the sum of my life be? And what risks was I willing to take to solve the equation?

Apparently God can use all things—including math—to prepare a hurried heart to respond to Him when He's about to do a new thing. If I hadn't been pondering the "value of x" for so many weeks after my brother's visit, I don't think I would have been ready for what followed.

In the middle of the night, Tony's former boss, Mad Dog, called from Wellington, New Zealand, to offer Tony a three-month position film editing at Jackamond Studios. Ever since the success of *The Lord of the Rings*, Wellington had become *the* location for up-and-coming filmmakers. Tony saw the job as the big break he had been waiting for. I saw it as an opportunity to step off the edge of my well-padded nest and take a free fall into the unknown.

After all, our daughter was in college, and we were no longer financially responsible for my mother-in-law's convalescent care. Tony and I could do this. We could leave everything for three months and have the exotic travel experience we had only dreamed about during our college days.

I always do my best thinking while shaving my legs in a tub full of bubbles. The two weeks prior to our departure for Wellington, I had the smoothest legs and the most wrinkled fingers in all of Los Angeles.

I'd thought through every detail and confidently arrived at the airport with everything I needed. Everything, that is, except one item I hadn't tucked in my suitcases or sent ahead in the boxes.

I didn't pack a single friend.

After spending most of my life in the same city, same church, and same circles, I suddenly was minus my built-in community of friends.

Looking back, I now see how unnatural it was to change a well-established migratory route in the middle of life and expect my wings to start flapping in rhythm as soon as I took the free fall. It shouldn't have been such a surprise that I fell so hard. After all, everything in my world had flip-flopped.

I think it was necessary, though, for me to tumble as far down under as I did. Otherwise, I never would have stumbled into the Chocolate Fish on a fine fall Friday in February with feathers in my hair. And that's where I found Jill.

If Jill were the one telling this story, she would say that's where she found *me*. But I'm saying that's where I found her. It had become clear that to solve the math problem written over this season of my life, I needed one more whole number. That little number was one. One new best friend. Jill.

Jill likes math. She sees math in art and nature and isn't afraid of the unknown equations. Two years ago when she and I stood in front of a painting at an Australian art museum in Sydney, she opened my eyes to the beauty of balance and symmetry, and that's when I began to make peace with math.

But before I flutter through our story, I will add one more important point. I believe the reason I found Jill wasn't so much because I was looking, but because she was waiting for me, hanging by her painted toenails on the edge of her own empty nest.

During the two weeks before we left for New Zealand, every day felt like a storm at sea. My husband turned into a ruthless commander, as the intensity of it all rose in tidal wave fashion and swept us through our final days in California. When the tsunami receded, I found myself washed up at an unfamiliar airport on the underside of the globe.

The only comforting sight was the grinning face of Tony's boss, Marcus, aka "Mad Dog," who met us at the baggage claim in Wellington. He punched Tony in the arm. "What did you think of that flight? Was I right about its being a marathon film fest? How many did you watch?"

"Five. No seven. No, I think it was five." Tony's adrenaline-induced gaze seemed frozen on his face.

Mad Dog adjusted his frayed corduroy cap. "Do you want to eat something first or go right to your new place?"

"Home," I said, as if it were a secret password that would lead me into this new world. All I needed was my new space around me so I could start fluffing up things the way I liked. Then I would be ready to remind myself why this had been a good decision.

"Home it is. Hope you guys like this place." Mad Dog loaded our luggage into the back of a van he had borrowed and off we went.

"We really appreciate all you did to find us a place. I'm

going to owe you big time." Suddenly Tony pointed to the roof of the terminal. "Hey, it's Gollum!" An enormous model of the bald, grim-faced Middle-earth icon peered down on us, looking like a gigantic alien that had fallen to earth and gotten his foot stuck through the roof.

"I guess we're not in Kansas anymore, Toto," I said.

Tony gave me a gratuitous wink at my attempt to make a joke. I gripped the car door's handle. Not because of Tony's wink or Gollum's glare, but because Mad Dog was driving on the left side of the road.

Tony laughed. "This is wild!"

"You'll get used to it," Mad Dog said. "Only took me a week when I moved here. Maybe less."

I expected an oncoming car to ram into us any moment. Everyone was going the opposite from what my brain said was correct. Mad Dog drove past a row of low-rise buildings, and I tried to take it all in. Stop lights, a normal-looking city bus, lots of small cars, billboards—and all of a sudden an Esprit store. All the evidences of Western civilization were here, yet it felt so different.

"There's the Embassy," Mad Dog said with reverence. He pointed to a pale yellow vintage square building. Fixed on the roof was another creature born in Tolkien's imagination. This one looked like a swooping black dragon with a long neck.

"How strange that the U.S. Embassy would have a dragon movie prop on top of it," I said.

Mad Dog and Tony both looked at me as if I were an alien creature who had just stuck my foot through the roof and landed in the same car with them.

"What?"

"Kathleen," Tony said patiently, "that's not the U.S. Embassy. That's the Embassy Theatre. And on the roof that's a fell beast ridden by a Ringwraith."

"Oh, yeah." I diverted my gaze out the window. I hoped I wouldn't be tested on any more *Lord of the Rings* trivia before we completed the last few miles of a very long journey to our new home.

We turned onto a narrow road and followed a pristine bay that skirted Wellington like a fancy azure petticoat. Thousands of houses dotted the low, rolling green hills that rose from the bay.

Fifteen minutes later, Mad Dog slowed the van as we entered a residential area. After several blocks, he stopped the car. "This is it. What do you think?"

I peered out the window at a bungalow-style house. The first thing I noticed was the grinning figurine standing his post in front of a narrow row of yellow and orange mums. I'd seen a number of lawn gnomes in my day and a pink flamingo or two, but this was the first ceramic hobbit I'd ever seen guarding a flower bed.

"Cute," I said with a smile. "But the hobbit definitely needs to go."

Mad Dog let out his guffaw laugh. "You'll have to clear that one with Mr. Barry, the landlord. What do you think of the garage?"

The tiny building that was separate from the main house had a window in front with curtains. It reminded me of the tool-shed my father had built in our backyard when I was a girl. My two sisters and I wanted to turn the shed into a playhouse, but Dad never let us.

"The garage is cute, too." I turned my attention to the main house. The bungalow appeared to be freshly painted in a soft shade of celery green with white trim around the two front windows. It was much smaller than our home in California, but I could make this cottage into "our" place for three months.

"You think this will work for you?" Mad Dog asked.

"Yes." I nodded and looked to see if Tony agreed. He did.

"You got a good woman, Tony." Mad Dog reached into the back of the van for our luggage. "Last week a guy who came down here from Canoga Park left after ten days on the job. His wife said she couldn't live in such primitive conditions. She said he had to decide between her or the job. He picked her."

"Good choice." I looped a shoulder bag over my arm and reached for another bag.

Mad Dog looked at me with his eyebrows raised. "If you say so."

I headed for the front door and was at the doorstep when Mad Dog called, "Kathleen, over here." He was standing by the garage's side door.

I stumbled through the grass and past the lantern-holding, smirking hobbit and wondered if the house key was hidden in the garage. Or maybe Mad Dog wanted to give us the full tour before we went inside the house.

He opened the garage's side door. Tony stepped in first. I followed, and the lights turned on. *The lights turned on.*

This was it. We were "home."

Barely breathing, I dropped both the shoulder bags and stood in the middle of our garage apartment. The single room came with a bed covered in an overly bright floral bedspread, a corner table, two metal patio chairs, a sink, an armchair, a hot plate, and the prized feature—a dorm-sized refrigerator.

"Bathroom is back there." Mad Dog pointed to a door that looked as if it should open to the backyard.

I looked at Tony. He wasn't moving. Or blinking.

With quiet steps, I wove my way through the furniture to the closed door and opened it. The newly built bathroom/laundry room/storage room/closet space was nearly half the size of the entire garage apartment. The room had been beautifully finished and was by far the nicest part of the apartment. The white curtains fluttered as a cool breeze came through the open window and coaxed me to breathe again.

I looked at the bathtub, my usual place of retreat and reflection in times of stress. The inner sanctum was defiled by a wooden drying rack propped up inside it. Over the rack was draped a pair of men's briefs. Not just any briefs, but giant-sized briefs.

The cry of distress that had been welling up inside me came out in two unexpected words. "Jumbo briefs!"

"What?" Tony came over to me.

I pointed and blinked so I wouldn't cry.

"Who would've left their underwear in here?" Tony asked.

"They look a little too large to belong to the garden hobbit," I said in a pathetically squeaky voice.

Mad Dog cracked up, his cough-laugh bouncing off the walls. "You keep that sense of humor going, Kathleen, and you'll be fine."

I pressed my lips together and felt my heart swell with empathy for the wife from Canoga Park. Perhaps she had been the tenant in this toolshed before us. Her departure might have been the reason Mad Dog was able to find a place for us. Perhaps the jumbo briefs were her husband's and had been left in their hasty departure.

Tony glanced my way. Our discussions about simplifying life during these three months had sounded so noble and appealing when we were in California working out a plan. We agreed that we needed to do this without the expense of a car. Obviously both of us thought the amount we had set aside for rent would have resulted in a lot more living space than it had.

How many days do we have before Tony starts work? Three? No, wait. What day is this?

We flew out of LAX on Tuesday night. We lost a day when we crossed the international date line, so that made today Thursday. At least I thought it was Thursday.

I am so lost. What are we doing here?